ALL THEY
Wanted

Wanted
BOOK SEVEN

GW00536854

NEW YORK TIMES & *USA TODAY* BESTSELLING AUTHOR
KELLY ELLIOTT

Copyright © 2016 by Kelly Elliott
Published by K. Elliott Enterprises

Cover design by Sara Eirew Photographer
Cover photo by Shannon Cain
http://photographybyshannoncain.com
Editor: Nichole Strauss with Insight Editing Services
Interior Designer: Julie Titus with JT Formatting

First Edition: December 2016
Library of Congress Cataloging-in-Publication Data
All They Wanted: a Novella (The Wanted Series, Book 7) – 1st ed
ISBN-13: 978-1-943633-25-8

For exclusive releases and giveaways signup for Kelly's newsletter at
www.kellyelliottauthor.com

TO EVERYONE WHO WANTED
MORE OF THE *WANTED* GANG.

THIS ONE IS FOR YOU.

Mark Peterson
Sue Peterson
Matthew Peterson
(Ari) Arianna (Peterson) Johnson
Hope Bennett
Noah Bennett
Jacob Bennett
Grace (Johnson) Bennett
Emma Morris
Jase Morris
Mason Morris
Taylor (Atwood) Morris
Brad Atwood
Amanda Atwood
Megan (Atwood) Bennett
Arabella Bennett
Charlotte Bennett
(Gray) Grayson Bennett
Mireya Johnson
Luke Johnson
Trey Johnson
(Jeff) Jefferson Johnson
(Libby) Isabella (Hayes) Johnson
Joshua Hayes
Sharon (Philip) Johnson
Brian Johnson
Heather (Lambert) Hayes
(Will) William Hayes
(Alex) Alexandra (Mathews) Hayes
Ellie (Johnson) Mathews
Dewey Rhodes
Aaron Rhodes
Drake Rhodes
Bayli Hayes
Joshua Hayes
Jessie (Rhodes) Reynolds
Scott Reynolds Sr.
Scott Reynolds Jr.
Bryce Reynolds
Melody Reynolds
Lauren (Reynolds) Mathews
Hunter Mathews
Anissa Mathews
Colt Mathews
Grace Mathews
Jack Mathews
(Gunner) Drew Garrett Mathews
Garrett Mathews
Emma Mathews
Jimmy Mathews

GUNNER

The sound of a truck pulled my attention away from the fence I was mending. Jeff parked and jumped out, wearing a huge grin. I'd seen that look on his face before. He had an idea, one I was either going to love or hate.

"What's up?" I asked going back to twisting the wire.

He handed me a beer and leaned against the pole. I reached for it and opened it. "What do you want, Johnson?"

Laughing, he tipped his hat and asked, "Now why do you think I want something?"

After taking a drink, I lifted my brow and held up the beer. "You showed up with beer. Let me also add you showed up right when we were done, asshole."

Jeff slapped me on the side of my arm, knocking me off my balance. Dewey reached out to steady me on my feet.

"Camping."

I gave Jeff a blank stare.

"What about it?"

"I think we should go on a couples camping trip. Me and Ari, you and Ellie, and Josh and Heather."

Turning, I gathered up my tools. "I don't think taking two kids under one on a camping trip would be my kind of fun, Jeff."

"No. Leave the kids. I'm talking Friday to Monday morning. Three nights only. I'm almost positive Ari and Ellie would be up for a few nights away from Alex and Luke. And I've already talked to Josh. He thinks Heather would be down for it."

Dewey and I both laughed. I shot a look at Dewey and we both shook our heads. "I think they would be up for a night away … in a bed and breakfast in Fredericksburg." Stopping what I was doing, I glanced back at him. "Have you forgotten, your wife is pregnant? And what's Josh thinking. Heather is pregnant with twins."

"So. They can't camp because they're pregnant? Besides, I've already mentioned it to Ari. She said as long as she has a cot or blow-up mattress and food, she's in."

Setting my tool bag in the back of my truck, I took my hat off and wiped away the evidence of my work. It was late April and already hot. This summer was going to be brutal.

"What about Brad and Amanda?"

"Brad said Amanda was too far along and would never be in the mood for camping."

With a sigh, I met Jeff's stare. He looked like a dog begging for food. "I'll talk to Ellie about it."

Jeff fist pumped. "Yes!"

"But … I'm not promising anything."

Pointing to me, Jeff walked backward to his truck. "I'm telling you, dude. This camping trip is going to go down in fucking history as the best camping trip of all time. And I happen to know, Ellie is going to be on board."

He opened the door to his truck. Clearly he and my wife had come up with this plan. Being married to my best friend's little sister always seemed to keep me on my toes. When the two of them came up with a plan, they banned together until the end.

"Oh, I have no doubt it will go down in history," I called out as he grinned and jumped into the truck. As he pulled off I turned to Dewey. "How do I get myself into this shit?"

He threw his head back and laughed his ass off. "Better you than me, Gunner. Better you than me."

"You really want to go camping, Ells?"

Ellie quietly shut Alex's door. She motioned for me to follow her downstairs.

Once we were in the kitchen, she pulled out an apple pie and cut a piece. "I think it would be fun, Gunner. Think about it, when was the last time we all got to hang out with no kids?" Glancing up at me, she gave me a sexy as hell look. "We can get drunk and have wild sex in our tent."

She licked apple off of her fingers and raised her brows. My dick jumped in my pants.

"It has been awhile."

A smile moved slowly across her face. "It has. Before Luke was born. Besides, after the girls have their babies, times like this will be gone. At least for a few years."

I nodded and leaned against the counter.

"Where should we go?"

Her face lit up. "Garner State Park."

"How did I know you were going to say that?"

"Come on, we've talked about camping there before and it's an amazing state park."

Jetting out her lower lip, she pouted. I couldn't help but smile at her attempt to get what she wanted. "Come here, Ells."

Her blue eyes lit up with desire. "Why, Mr. Mathews, are you wanting to mess around?"

"With my beautiful wife? Hell yeah I am."

Ellie walked up to me and placed her hands on my chest. "I would so be stripping out of my clothes right now ... but your parents are on their way over."

My mouth dropped. "What? Why?"

Cocking her head to the side, Ellie shrugged. "Not sure. They mentioned wanting to stop by later this evening to talk to us."

A sick feeling washed over me. Ellie noticed. "Don't think like that, Gunner. I'm sure everything is fine."

Cupping her face with my hands, I gazed into those blue eyes. "Have I told you how much I love you lately?"

"Not in the last few minutes."

The left side of my mouth rose into a smile. "Let me fix that," I whispered while I gently brushed my lips across hers.

Ellie's hands grabbed onto my arms. Moving my lips to her ear, I softly repeated, "I love you."

I ran my nose along her neck, eliciting a small moan from her. "Mmm ... you're tempting me, Mr. Mathews."

"You always tempt me, sweetheart."

A light knock on the back door had me pulling away. Ellie pouted then winked. "Later?"

"You better believe later."

Ellie made her way to the back door and opened it with a huge grin on her face. "Hi, Jack and Grace!"

My parents walked in and each kissed Ellie on the cheek. "Hi, darling. How are you feeling?"

"I'm feeling wonderful!" Ellie responded.

Reaching my hand out, my father and I shook hands first before he pulled me into a quick hug. One good slap on the back and he took a seat at the table.

"Hey, Mom," I said with a smile and drew her in for a hug.

She sat next to my father and gazed up at me with a smile. "Hello, darling."

Ellie put the apple pie in the middle of the table with a few plates. "Homemade apple pie if anyone wants a piece."

Of course my father immediately dug in. "Well, I was raised to never turn down homemade apple pie."

A smile tugged at Ellie's mouth. "And it's Gram's recipe."

With a laugh, my father responded, "Even better." No one could ever pass up something that Grams had created in the kitchen. Not even her own son.

I took a seat and looked between my parents. "So, what brings the two of you over here, and after Alex is asleep?"

Folding her hands neatly across her lap, my adorable mother flashed a huge grin.

"Well, your father and I wanted to talk to you both about something."

I lifted my brow. "Sounds serious."

"Well no, it's not really too serious."

Ellie took the seat next to me. I reached for her hand and held it as I watched my father shovel in the apple pie as fast as he could. "That pie good, Dad?"

"Mmm hmm. Don't tell, Mom, but I think you have mastered the recipe, Ellie."

Ellie squeezed my hand. Glancing to her, I couldn't help but smile as her eyes lit up with happiness. She was so damn beautiful.

And mine.

Dad sighed and pushed the plate away from him. "So anyway, kids, let's get right to it."

I motioned for him to keep talking.

"Grace, would you like me to be the one to ask?"

My mother nodded.

"Drew, Ellie, we love spending time with Alex. Beyond words love it. Now we know she is four months and that is young. But, we'd love to be able to have her spend some more time with us. Maybe spend the night again. We had so much fun with her."

I couldn't help notice how my mom was looking between Ellie and me. Waiting to see our reaction. There would be no way Ellie and I would ever deny my parents time with Alex. I wanted my daughter to have the same relationship with her grandparents as I did with Grams and Gramps.

With a huge grin, Ellie said, "There isn't anyone I would trust our daughter to be with more than you two."

My mother returned Ellie's smile. "That makes me so happy! We thought maybe if y'all would like to get things caught up around the ranch, or the house."

"How about for the weekend?" Ellie blurted out.

"What do you mean for the weekend? Keep Alex for a whole weekend?" My parents turned and gave each other goofy as hell smiles.

"Yes!" they both said at once.

I could hear the excitement in their voices.

Ellie turned to me and simply said, "No more excuses. We're going camping."

Two

ELLIE

"Are you sure Gunner volunteered to bring *all* of the food?" Heather asked. Her brows were furrowed.

"Yep. He planned out the meals for the entire weekend, and Jeff agreed to be the cook."

Ari groaned. "He does realize he has two pregnant women to feed, right?"

I chuckled. "He's well aware of that, y'all."

I'd never seen anyone with the food cravings while pregnant like Heather and Ari. And when they were together, it was worse. Almost as if their obsession with food combined with one another.

Heather roamed through the cots. "There are so many cots."

"You're getting a cot?" Ari asked Heather.

Heather rolled her eyes. "If I thought for one moment Josh would let me get a cot, I'd be all over it."

"This is going to be fun. You'll see."

Ari narrowed her eyes at me. "Why are you and Jeff so game on this camping trip?"

"I don't know," I stated with a shrug. "It kind of feels like this is our last big fling if you will. Once you have another baby and Heather has the twins, our time together as a group will be cut in half."

Heather gave me a warm smile. "But we'll still be together. It will just be play dates."

"I know that. There's no way for me to easily explain it, but I really feel like we all need this weekend."

Hooking her arm with mine, Ari winked. "If this trip ends up being miserable as hell … which I'm not saying it will, but if it does. You're to blame."

"Gee, thanks. Come on, let's go feed those babies."

Heather picked up her pace. "Good, because I'm starving. I want enchiladas."

Ari gasped. "Yes! Enchiladas. That sounds yummy."

After dropping Heather and Ari back home, I took a few minutes to clear my head before I pulled up to the house. I wasn't sure what was wrong with me, but whatever it was, I needed to snap out of it. Grace said I probably was still suffering from baby blues. I was happy … yet sad. I couldn't explain it.

Grabbing some bags, I headed into the house. "Gunner?" I called out into the empty house.

I set the bags on the counter and reached for my phone to call him.

It only rang twice before he answered. "Hey, sweetheart. You back from Austin?"

A warmth spread across my body simply from hearing his voice. Even after being married for almost two years, he still made my heart flutter. Smiling, I answered him, "I am. Where are you and my sweet baby girl?"

"Mom and Dad's place. I figured when you got back you might like a bit of time to yourself. I set everything out for you to take a nice hot bath."

Thud. There went my heart. *How did I ever get so lucky with this man?*

I headed into our bedroom. "That sounds amazing. How's Alex?"

"She's being loved on like you wouldn't believe."

"Awe, I bet she is." I walked into the bathroom and stopped. Candles were everywhere. Next to the window sat a fresh bouquet of daises that Gunner must have gotten from the garden. A towel along with a bath bomb sat on the edge of the soaker tub.

"Gunner, it looks like a romantic spa in here."

The sound of a screen shutting told me he had stepped outside. "Good. Now strip out of your clothes and get in that tub. I'll be heading back soon and putting Alex down. She's exhausted from all of the attention she's gotten from everyone."

"Everyone?"

"I took her to see Grams and Gramps before stopping here. Poor little thing barely had a nap."

Chewing on my lip, I imagined Gunner in the tub with me. "Should I wait? I'd love to have you join me in this oversized tub of ours."

A screen door slammed again. "Let me get our daughter. I'm coming home now."

My hand covered my mouth to hide my laughter. I heard Gunner tell his parents he was leaving. "Sorry, Mom and Dad. Ellie really wants to see Alex before she goes to bed."

I shook my head. "You totally pinned that all on me."

"Yep. See ya in a few, sweetheart."

The phone went dead. Pulling it back, I shook my head and headed back to the kitchen. I searched for the perfect bottle of wine before grabbing two glasses and the plate of fruit and cheese I quickly made up.

The sound of Gunner's truck pulling up had me rushing back into the master bathroom to drop everything off before heading back to the kitchen.

Gunner walked in with our sleeping daughter in his arms and my libido shot through the roof. Never mind the fact that my husband was drop-dead gorgeous, or that his blue eyes seemed to be sparkling, it was the site of him carrying out daughter in his arms that got to me the most.

"Hey," he softly said before kissing me on the lips.

"I missed you today," I replied as I handed him a bottle I'd gotten ready.

"I missed you too. Let's take care of the princess here so I can give my queen some one-on-one attention."

The pull in my lower stomach was hard to miss. The only thing I could do was nod. Gunner turned and headed toward the stairs. My hand went to my stomach to settle the butterflies flying about.

Tears formed in my eyes as my emotions took over. I never in my life dreamed I would ever be this happy.

Dragging in a deep breath, I headed to Alex's room.

I stood outside of the room and watched as Gunner hummed softly while feeding our precious baby.

He glanced up at me and smiled. Those dimples made my heart flutter. "What are you thinking, Ells?"

I didn't even need to think of my response. "How I'm the luckiest woman on earth."

Gunner winked. "And soon to be the most satisfied."

I was the luckiest woman on earth, no doubt.

Three

JEFF

Tossing the last bag into the back of my truck, I turned and grabbed the tent. Setting it next to the giant ass bag Ari had packed, I let out a sigh. I still couldn't believe she packed so many things.

"Hey, cowboy."

I spun around to see my beautiful bride sitting on top of Big Roy. I hated that she rode while being pregnant, but I knew Ari. It wouldn't matter how much I didn't want her to do it. If she wanted to, she'd do it.

"Hey, beautiful. How's he feel?"

Ari laughed. "Slow. Lazy bastard doesn't want to move. I've never ridden a horse that walks this slow in my entire life. If I didn't know any better, I'd swear you had a heart-to-heart with him."

She raised a brow and stared at me.

"I might have given him a few extra oats and told him I'd put an AC in his stall if he went easy on you."

Ari slid off of Roy and let him graze. "You know we can't keep him here, Jeff. He's Gunner's horse."

With a shrug, I pulled her to me. "I already talked to Gunner about it. If you insist on riding, Big Roy is staying here. He had no problem with it. Besides, they live ten minutes from us."

Shaking her head, Ari lifted her hand and traced my jaw with her finger. "I love that you worry about me, but I promise I'll be careful."

My chest ached with the memory of Ari losing our first baby. "I can't help but worry."

Sadness filled her eyes. "I know, babe. But we can't stress out the entire time. We'll get through this by the grace of God."

My hand covered hers. "Do you have any idea how much I love you?"

Her eyes lit up. "I may have some idea, but you could show me."

Wiggling my eyebrows, I picked her up while she let out a scream.

"What about Big Roy?" she called out.

"Damn it."

Turning, I headed back and grabbed his reins. A car came down the driveway, causing me to let out a moan.

"Son-of-a-bitch. Why are they back so soon?"

Ari slapped my chest. "Put me down, Jeff. My father's gonna know what we were doing."

I slowly set her on the ground. "Like I care what your dad thinks."

With a smirk, Ari gave me a *really* look. "Uh-huh. Sure you don't care. The moment he gets out of the car I know what you're going to do."

"Tell him he interrupted my special attention time."

Her head jerked back. "Your what?"

Mark pulled up and honked the horn, prompting me to turn and quickly take Big Roy into the barn.

"I knew it!" Ari shouted.

Turning to Big Roy, I gave him a pat. "We're not stupid, are we boy?"

The moment I stepped into the house, I knew I had made a mistake.

"Arianna, are you sure going on a camping trip is such a great idea?"

Ari's father was at it again. I swore he only did this because Ari told him it was my idea to go camping.

"Why would it be a bad idea, Dad?"

Mark glared at me. "You're pregnant for one."

I smiled weakly. "I'll be sure she is spoiled and well taken care of, sir."

"Damn right you will."

Ari walked up to her father. "Dad, stop it. If I didn't want to go, I wouldn't. Besides, y'all are going to have Luke for the entire weekend."

Mark sighed. "You don't have to go out of town for us to keep our grandson."

Sue sat quietly while she fed Luke oatmeal.

"You're still planning on staying here, right? I mean, Luke will be more comfortable in his own bed," Ari stated as she glanced between her parents.

Facing Ari, Sue answered, "Of course we are. It will be nice to spend some time in the fresh country air as well as see Jack and Grace."

"Where are you going to sleep?" Mark blurted out.

"In a tent," I replied.

He glared at me. "No shit. Where is my daughter sleeping? On the hard ground?"

"Dad!" Ari cried out. "Stop being so mean."

"I'm not being mean. The boy promised to take care of you, and I want to know how he plans on making *you* comfortable during this little camping trip."

It was then Mark glanced down at my T-shirt and rolled his eyes. Taking a quick peek, I read my shirt.

"That's probably the most accurate shirt I've ever seen you wear."

"Daddy, please!" Ari pleaded.

"We'll have a blow-up mattress, Mark. I've made sure that Ari will not want for anything on this trip."

Mark huffed as Matt came walking into the kitchen eating an apple. He smiled when he saw me.

"Hey, assmole."

"Matt!" Sue and Ari said at once.

With a huge grin, I replied to Matt, "Hey, buddy. You want to see the horses?"

He nodded and handed his apple to Mark. "Here, Dad. I'm going to go learn to be a mudder-fucking cowboy."

Mark groaned and it was everything I could do to not laugh. Ari flashed me a dirty look that was quickly replaced by a smile when I winked at her.

"For Christ's sake. Don't teach him any more of your special words, Jeff!" Mark called out.

I lifted my hand and replied, "I'll try not to!"

Before the screen door shut, I heard Mark ask, "Why did you marry that boy? Why?"

With a wide grin, I glanced down to Matt. "Buddy, this is your time. What do you want to do?"

Matt's smile spread from ear to ear. "I want to be just like you!"

I nodded. "Sounds good to me. That ought to make your dad really happy."

Four

ARI

The smell of bacon filled the air as I made my way into Luke's room. Slowly opening the door, I grinned when I saw him sitting in his crib. "Good morning, handsome boy."

He smiled and called out, "Mama!"

I never knew I could love someone like I loved Luke. He was my entire world. Reaching into the crib, I picked him up. "Let's get you all cleaned up and join Daddy downstairs for breakfast."

"Dada!" Luke yelled out. Kissing him on the cheek, I grinned. "But who is the boss?" I whispered.

Luke let out a sweet laugh. "Mama!"

Tickling his stomach, I nodded. "That's right. Mommy is always in charge."

My little happy man laughed the entire time I changed him and got him dressed. Holding him close to me, I headed downstairs. He was growing up so fast and now that he was full-on walking, he was every-where. I took full advantage of the moments he let me hold him.

The smell of bacon and pancakes filled the air. Rounding the corner and heading into the kitchen, I came to a stop.

"Hey, Ari."

"Dad, what are you doing here?"

Jeff turned and looked at me with a frown on his face. "He decided to show up early and hang with me some today."

Pressing my lips tightly together, I attempted not to chuckle. "Oh. Um. Why?"

Luke cried out for my father and he quickly made his way over to me. He took Luke from my arms and proceeded to fly him around like he was an airplane.

"Do I need a reason to spend time with my family?"

"Yes," Jeff mumbled. I pointed to him with my brows furrowed and mouthed *stop*. Jeff and my father had been at odds with each other since day one. Daddy didn't think Jeff was good enough for me and Jeff swore up and down the only goal in life my father had was to take him out. Deep down, I knew they both loved each other but were too damn stubborn to admit it.

"No, of course you don't need a reason, Daddy."

Taking off into the living room, Jeff started shaking the spatula at me. "Why is he here and why does he want to hang with me today?"

I shrugged and whispered, "I don't know. Maybe he wants to get to know you better?"

"Ha! He's trying to get my schedule down so he can hire someone to take me out! He's been waiting patiently all this time and now he's ready to make the hit."

My hands went to my hips. "Really, Jeff? Take you out? Make. The. Hit?"

Jeff pinned me with his eyes. He looked so serious I couldn't help but laugh. "You're ridiculous, Jeff," I said as I got Luke's breakfast ready.

Dad walked back into the kitchen with Luke and proceeded to put him in his highchair.

"I think the little guy is ready to eat."

With a grin, I handed the bowl of oatmeal and bananas to my father.

"So, are you kids packed up and ready to go?"

Jeff placed a plate full of bacon, and another with pancakes on it, in the middle of the table. For some reason with this pregnancy, I craved both all the time. "We are. I got everything packed up yesterday. The truck is ready to go."

"Did you get both of my cases?" I asked with a sweet smile.

Rolling his eyes, Jeff replied, "I did. But you do know we're only gone for three nights, right?"

"You never know. They have dance parties at Garner!"

My father chuckled. "Camping with you was always … fun."

I sat and made a plate while Jeff did the same. "Where's Mom and Matt?"

"They stayed at the hotel in Fredericksburg so Matt could swim in the indoor pool this morning."

Jeff cleared his throat. "And look at you, up all bright and early."

With a smirk, my father replied, "Well, if I'm going to be playing you for a few days, I need to know your routine in and out. What is it you do every day, Jeff?"

When Jeff's head snapped up, I had to fight hard to keep my composure. His eyes widened as he glared at me and mouthed, *I told you so.* He motioned his throat being cut and all I could do was shake my head and look away.

A small part of me wondered if what my father was doing was exactly what Jeff was saying.

Glancing back at my dad, he was smiling and talking to Luke. He was a giant teddy bear. No way.

He stopped and shot a dirty look over to Jeff for no reason at all. My stomach dropped.

He wouldn't. Would he? No.

Looking back at my father, I gave him a long hard look.

No. He wouldn't.

"Ari, we have to go."

I hugged Luke one more time. "Mommy loves you, buddy! I'm going to miss you so much!"

Jeff moved in and kissed Luke on the cheek and gave him another hug. "We're going to be late, Ari. If we want to get set up before dark, we have to leave now."

"Mom, we're just under two hours away so if you need anything, you'll text me, right?"

"Yes, Ari, I've raised two kids and I've watched this handsome boy plenty of times. Go and have fun."

I nodded. "We are going to have fun!"

"Good, because once this baby comes, the fun is over."

My smile dropped. "What?"

Pushing me toward the truck, my mother replied, "I'm kidding. Sort of."

"Well that makes me feel all warm and fuzzy, Mom."

Jeff opened my door for me as I climbed in. Reaching in, my father gave me a kiss. "Don't worry about Luke, sweetheart. He'll have so much fun he won't even notice you're gone."

A sinking feeling in my heart hit me. I was going to miss him so much. "O-okay."

"And don't worry about the horses. I followed Jeff around and I've got it. Seems easy enough to do."

Jeff huffed as he climbed into the driver's seat. "Easy enough my ass," Jeff spoke under his breath.

"Plus, Scott's going to be stopping by each morning and evening. Turns out your husband doesn't trust me to do the job."

With a fake grin, Jeff stated, "He said it not me."

Jerking my head over to Jeff, I said, "Stop already." I looked back at my father. "Thanks, Daddy. I love y'all. Hey, where's Matt?"

"He's napping. All the swimming this morning wore him out," my mother replied.

With a slight frown, I nodded. "Okay. Well we're leaving I guess. Tell him bye and I love him. Hope he has fun here!"

Jeff started the truck.

"Be safe driving," my father said as he pointed to Jeff. "If anything happens to my baby, I'm coming after you."

I shook my head and turned to Jeff. He had a look of total fear on his face. "Right. We're off."

Daddy stepped away from the truck. I waved and shouted, "Bye, Luke! Be a good boy! I love you!"

Luke waved and blew kisses to us as we drove off.

I watched them until Jeff turned and headed down the driveway. My heart felt heavy.

"Jeff," I whispered.

Taking my hand in his, he gently kissed the back of it. "He's going to be fine, baby. We'll be back Monday morning. Just think, it's just us. No getting up early, no middle of the night diaper changes. Just you and me naked in a tent all weekend."

There was no denying the ache between my legs. "No Gramps walking in on us."

"Hell yes!" Jeff shouted. He squeezed my hand. "The things I'm going to do to you tonight."

I ran my tongue along my lips. I ached to feel Jeff against my body. A part of me longed for the days when we could strip down and have sex any time and anywhere we wanted. Now it seemed like we both collapsed into bed with exhaustion, a good night kiss was the only action we saw on those days.

"You're right. This weekend is going to be magical."

"Yes it is, baby. A weekend to remember."

Five

JOSH

I inhaled a deep breath and slowly let it out. The cool spring air felt good in my chest. Heather popped out of the tent with a huge smile on her face. Her hand rested on her swollen stomach. My heart felt as if it would burst I was so damn happy.

"You've got a big smile on your face."

Reaching for her hands, I drew her in closer to me. "That's because I'm happy. I don't think I've ever been this happy before, Heather."

With a light chuckle, she shook her head. "I didn't realize you liked camping so much."

I placed my hand on the side of her face as she gently leaned into it. Her eyes sparkled while she searched my face. "It's being with you. *You* make me happy, princess." My other hand rested on her stomach. "Baby one and baby two make me happy too."

She rolled her eyes and let out a light-hearted sigh. "You can't keep calling them that, Josh."

Slipping my hand behind her neck, I kissed her gently. It would be easy to get lost in the kiss had it not been for someone honking their damn horn.

"Jeff and Ari are here," Heather softly spoke against my lips.

"I hear."

"Let the party begin!" Jeff shouted as I glanced over my shoulder at him hanging out of his truck.

Heather chuckled. "I'm going to finish getting things set up. You should go help Jeff so Ari doesn't try to."

"Do I get a kiss before I leave?"

"Of course, even though you're only going to be a few feet away."

Reaching on her toes, Heather gave me a quick peck on the lips. "I love you."

"I love you too, princess. Don't lift anything, okay?"

Her smile made her blue eyes sparkle. "I promise I won't."

Jeff was already pulling everything out of the back of his truck when I walked over to their site. Gunner and Ellie's site was in the middle of the other two sites. We were situated at the end of the road, so it was perfect.

He stopped and reached for my hand to shake it. "Dude. These campsites are perfect."

"You do realize you picked them out right, Jeff?"

With a wide grin, he nodded. "Hell yeah I do. They're wide enough apart for privacy and close to the river."

"Hey, Josh!"

I glanced over my shoulder to see Ari walking up with a huge smile on her face.

"Hey, pretty momma. You look great, Ari."

Her face blushed, which was rare for Ari. "Thanks! I feel amazing. Starving though. Jeff wouldn't stop because he wanted to beat Gunner here."

I chuckled while I spread the tent out. "Well, y'all did. Last I heard Gunner and Ellie were running late. Alex was fussy then a couple cows got out in the road and they had to get them."

"Damn, that sucks. Which fence was down?" Jeff asked while we both assembled the tent.

With a shrug, I responded, "Not sure. He didn't say. The only thing he said was he was rushing to get out the door and on the road."

"Did y'all know they had miniature golf?" Heather asked while walking up.

"Oh, my gosh! I swear in just a day you've gotten bigger, Heather!" Ari gasped.

It wasn't lost on me, and I'm sure not on Ari either, that Heather flashed her a go-to-hell look. Ari was a little bit further along than Heather, but Heather was showing a lot more than Ari was.

"Two babies, Ari. I've got two baking in there."

Ari's smile faded some before returning. "You look beautiful, Heather. Your skin is glowing."

With a wink, Heather replied, "Nice save."

It didn't take us long to get Ari and Jeff's campsite up and ready. Jeff bitched the entire time he carried both of Ari's suitcases over to the tent.

"You never know what I'm going to need. They have nightly dances here at the park. I need to look good."

Jeff popped out of the tent. "For who?"

With a come hither look, Ari responded, "Why you of course."

Rolling his eyes, Jeff pulled out his phone. "Where in the hell are Gunner and Ellie?"

Not two seconds later, Gunner pulled into their campsite.

"Jesus, Mary, and Joseph. It's about damn time! I need steak!" Ari cried out.

The four of us made our way over to Gunner's truck. The second he stepped out, Ari asked about food while Gus rushed out of the truck and started smelling everything in sight.

"Did you bring fruit?"

With a nod of his head, Gunner grinned. "I certainly did."

"Kiwi?" Ari asked with a lifted brow.

"Yes, I got your damn kiwi, Ari."

She did a little jump and joined Heather and Ellie as Gus circled them looking for a treat. With a quick pat on the head, Gus sank to the ground at Ellie's feet.

"Had a loose cow, huh?" Jeff asked.

With a frustrated groan, Gunner wiped his forehead then put his baseball cap on and shook his head. "Loose cow, fussy baby that Ellie didn't want to leave, a wreck that blocked the road for forty minutes, and a flat tire two miles from the park's fucking entrance. And to think I didn't even want to come camping."

I couldn't help but laugh. "Don't be that way. You know you want to spend some time with Ellie and let loose."

Gunner grunted, which was his way of saying he really did want to go camping.

"Let's hope that was the only hiccup because honestly, I don't think I can handle anything else. Ellie has been a basket case since we left and this was her idea! To top it off, she begged to bring Gus."

With a chuckle, Jeff shook his head and slapped the shit out of Gunner on the back. "Damn, luck is not on your side tonight."

"No, it's not," Gunner huffed as he headed to the back of his truck.

"I'll get the grill going at our campsite. We've got the table set up and everything's ready to go. Ari and Heather keep talking about steaks, so I say we grill that tonight."

"Sounds good," Gunner mumbled.

I shook my head and smiled. As much as Gunner was acting like he was pissed about this camping trip, he wanted to come like the rest of us did. Calling out to a retreating Jeff, I said, "I'll help Gunner get the food and then help set up."

Before I headed over to help Gunner, Ari and Heather called me over to read something.

Walking over to them, Ari shoved a map in my direction. "What does that say?"

I glanced down at it. "Trails map?"

"No, right there," Ellie said pointing to the top of the map.

"Geocache?"

"Yes! Ari and Heather won't do it!"

Ari placed her hands on her hips. "Keep reading."

I cleared my throat as I looked between the three of them. Glancing back at the map, I read, "Discover what geocaching is all about. Ages 10 and up."

"There. It's for kids, Ellie!" Ari argued.

Stomping her foot, Ellie cried out, "It's not! It looks like fun! We can pick up a list of real geocaches hidden in the park. Come on, y'all! We can call it practice for when we do it with the kids."

"I'm in," Heather said with a smile. Ari twisted around and glared at Heather.

"Um, Josh? Can you help me over here?" Gunner asked as he looked around the back of his truck.

I glanced back at Gunner. "Shit, yeah sorry." Jogging over, I stopped at the back of his truck. Something wasn't right because Gunner looked sick. His face was white as a ghost and he was trying to drag in deep breaths.

"What's wrong?" I asked.

Scrubbing both hands down his face, he moaned. "I fucked up so bad. So ... so ... bad."

Laughing, I said, "It can't be *that* bad."

His hands dropped to the side of his face. "Oh, it's bad, dude. I forgot the coolers of food."

My smile instantly dropped. "I'm sorry. I thought you said you forgot the food."

Nodding, he replied in a barely there whisper. "I did. That's what I said. We don't have any food."

"Gunner, no. How in the hell do you forget the one thing you were supposed to bring!"

"Shut up! You're going to cause a panic among the hungry pregnant women and then we're all done for!"

25

I quickly glanced over to the girls. They were still arguing about the damn geocache bullshit. Looking at Gunner, I said, "Do you have any idea what Ari and Heather are going to do to you when they find out you have no food! No kiwi or steak."

Gunner swallowed hard. "Oh shit. Ari's going to cut my balls off."

"I'm pretty sure she'll do more than that."

Covering his junk with his hands, Gunner groaned. "Shit! They're walking this way! What do we do?"

"We?" I said with a laugh. "Oh, hell no. You're on your own with this one."

Narrowing his eyes, he shot me a dirty look. "You bastard. You're gonna leave me out to hang? Alone?"

The girls stopped in front of us. Each surveying the scene before their eyes.

Ari lifted her brow as she wore an inquisitive look.

"She knows," I whispered.

Gunner hit my arm. "No, she can't."

"Josh and I need to run to the ... um ... to the store."

My head jerked to look at him. "What?"

"What for? We have enough food for a week," Ellie replied.

Ellie's phone beeped and she lifted it. "It's a text from your mom. Tell Drew he forgot to bring the two—"

Her eyes swung over to Gunner. She wore a horrified expression. "Gunner. You didn't."

Hitting him on the back, I laughed. "Oh, yes he did. Let the fun begin."

GUNNER

"One job. You had *one* job."

I pushed the cart down the aisle and tried not to listen to Ari.

"How in the hell do you forget to pack two giant containers of food? How?"

One. Two. Three. Deep breath in. Let it out.

"I could see forgetting your clothes. But the food? Really, Gunner?"

Four. Five. Six.

"He's not even paying any attention to me," Ari said as she threw in three bags of chips then totally had a mood shift. Clapping, she grinned wide and stated, "Oh, sloppy joes sound good!"

"Yeah, those do sound good!" Ellie agreed while looking at me and shrugging.

"I thought she wanted steaks?" I asked with a puzzled look.

Ari turned and pointed to me. "Hey, I want those too."

Thank goodness there was an HEB close by or we would have been living off of snacks from the park store.

I watched as Ari, Heather, and Ellie loaded up the cart almost to the max. I knew camping brought out the munchies in all of us, especially with Heather and Ari being pregnant. Their love of certain foods certainly grew the last few months. But with the way they were loading up the cart, you'd think they were afraid we would run out of food.

"Y'all do know we're only there for a few days right?" I asked.

Three heads turned and glared at me. "But Josh and Jeff do eat a lot of food," I quickly added. Ari grinned and Ellie scrunched her nose up while walking over to me. Leaning in, she gently kissed my cheek. "Good save, babe."

"Well, I was about to be shred to pieces by two hungry pregnant women."

Ellie giggled and headed back over to the girls. After checking out, I loaded the new ice chest I had bought down with ice and filled it with the food. The girls were in the truck as I walked the cart back to the store.

Hitting Jeff's number, I sighed.

"You get some food?"

"Yes. And now I have a new ice chest as well."

The asshole laughed. Some friends I had. "Should I fire up the pit?"

"Yes, and for your sake, I hope you can turn up the heat and cook these bitches fast. Ari is about to rip my head off."

"Just give her a Snickers bar. It's her pregnancy weakness."

"Ah, that explains the giant bag she threw in the cart."

Jeff chuckled. "I'm surprised she only put one bag in."

"Luckily I had a gut feeling and threw two more bags into the cart."

"Smart move."

I let out a light-hearted laugh. "We're on our way back."

"Good luck."

Stepping into the truck, I took a peek into the back seat to see both Ari and Heather breaking pieces off of a loaf of French bread.

With a soft groan, I turned back and started the truck. "I'm gonna need it if they run out of bread."

The small area we sat in was illuminated by the blazing fire. The warmth felt good as it hit my face. I drew Ellie in closer to me as she nestled her head against my chest.

"This is perfect," she whispered.

I kissed the top of her head and agreed. "It was a good idea, I'll admit."

She lifted her head and gave me that sweet smile of hers.

"All right, story time," Jeff said standing.

Rolling my eyes, I spoke, "And there went the peacefulness."

Ellie playfully hit me on the stomach while Jeff called Gus over to the sit next to him.

Jeff rubbed his hands together and looked around at everyone. "We can't roast marshmallows and sit around a fire without a ghost story."

"I love ghost stories!" Ellie replied as she snuggled in closer to me. The warmth of her body caused mine to come to life. I fought the desire to pick her up and carry her back to our tent and make love to her. I knew this was what she wanted for now, and I would be content with it. At least for a little while.

Jeff turned on the flashlight and stuck it under Gus' face.

"There ronce rwas a rory about a roung girl."

My jaw fell to the ground as Jeff continued to talk like Scooby-fucking-Doo.

"Dude, why in the hell are you talking like that?" Josh asked as Heather hit him on the arm.

Ari giggled. "He's talking like Scooby Doo. Because Gus is telling the story … get it?"

Josh's forehead furrowed as he looked between Jeff, Ari, and Heather. "I get the reference, but there are no kids around."

Jeff laughed. "Jesus, Josh. That's how dogs talk."

Now it was my turn to laugh. "Scrappy Doo doesn't talk like that."

Jeff's mouth opened to speak, then he shut it and sent me a glaring look. "Let me tell the damn story the way I want to tell it, will ya?"

I held up my hands in defeat while Josh lost it laughing.

"Well now I'm not in the mood to tell the story," Jeff said while turning off the flashlight.

Josh leaned toward the fire. "Dude, are you pouting right now?"

"Fuck you, Josh," Jeff spit out.

Ari stood up. "All right boys, let's not act like we're children. It's time to bring the adults hiding in you back out."

Ellie covered her mouth to hide her chuckle.

Ari continued to speak. "I say we play truth or dare!"

I groaned and shook my head. "Seriously, Ari? You just told us to grow up and now you want to play truth or dare?"

Her hands went to her hips and I knew this was one battle I wasn't going to attempt to fight.

"Truth or dare sounds like fun," I quickly added.

Ari wore a huge smile. "I thought so, Mathews."

Seven

ELLIE

couldn't help but giggle as I watched Gunner agree with Ari that truth or dare would be fun.

Leaning closer to him, I whispered, "Smart man."

"Did you see the death stare she shot me?"

Laughing, I replied, "I was afraid for you."

"I was afraid for my balls she was about to grab and twist," Gunner stated with a wink.

Ari clapped her hands to get everyone's attention.

"All right, y'all. Who wants to go first?"

I glanced around and no one raised their hands. Ari tilted her head and wore an evil grin. "Fine, no volunteers for truth or dare, so I'll pick who goes first."

She narrowed in on Josh. "Josh, you're up first."

Jerking his head back, Josh asked, "Me? Why me?"

"Oh, you know why," Ari stated as her brows drew together.

"Wasn't that in a movie? What was that movie called?" Heather asked while looking around at each of us. She didn't even seem to care that Josh wore a scared as hell expression on his face.

Gunner leaned in and softly spoke while staring at Josh. "Poor bastard. I wonder what she's going to make him do, because you know the stupid ass will pick dare and Ari knows it."

I instantly felt sorry for Josh because I knew Gunner was right.

Sitting up straighter, Josh put on a brave face. "I'll go first and I pick dare."

"Told you," Gunner said with a chuckle.

I don't think I've ever seen Ari smile that big before. She turned on her heels and walked over to the ice chests. Lifting the lid, she pulled out a bag and Heather and I gasped.

"Oh. No," Heather said.

Spinning around, Ari walked back over to Josh.

"Eat seven of these without taking a drink of water."

I was almost positive Josh was already starting to sweat.

"Peppers?" Josh asked while swallowing hard.

"Is he already sweating?" Jeff asked with a full-on laugh.

Ari pushed the bag closer to him. "What's the matter, Hayes. You afraid to eat a few jalapeño?"

"A few? Two would be a few, Ari. You said seven."

Looking around, Ari said, "Looks like we have our first failed dare for the night."

Josh grabbed the bag from Ari and opened it.

"Josh! You hate spicy things!" Heather cried out.

Standing, Josh gave Heather a reassuring look. "I've got this, princess."

Heather looked at me with wide eyes and a dropped mouth. We both knew, he so didn't have this.

"This should be fun," Gunner said while taking a drink from his beer.

I gripped Gunner's leg while I watched Josh reach in for a pepper.

"Seven. One right after the other," Ari confirmed again.

A look of horror washed over my face when Josh quickly popped the whole pepper into his mouth and chewed. He reached in for another and repeated the same action for seven peppers.

"Holy shit. He's crying!" Jeff cried out as he laughed hysterically.

"Oh, Josh," Heather said as she rushed over to him with a bottle of water.

Josh grabbed the water and downed it. "Fire. On. Fire. Gonna die. Help … me."

Gunner jumped up with another bottle of water. Snatching it from his hands, Josh drank it so fast he was spilling it all over himself.

"Can't breathe!" Josh hissed while drinking yet another bottle. "Bread! Something! Help!"

Ari let out a contented sigh. "I didn't think you had it in you, Hayes."

Josh glared at Ari while Heather handed him another bottle. Pointing to Ari, Josh said, "I hate you right now."

With a half pout, half smile, Ari replied, "Awe, you don't mean that, buttercup!"

Josh downed a beer. "My shit's gonna burn for weeks."

It was then everyone lost it laughing, including Josh.

Pulling my knees up to my chest, I smiled as I looked around the fire at my friends. They were more than friends. They were my family and I loved them. I was going to cherish this weekend forever.

Soft breath hit my neck, rousing me from my sleep. "Hey, sweetheart. You fell asleep."

Sitting up, I stretched and let out a long yawn. "Gosh, I was tired," I replied while looking around the fire. "Where is everyone?"

"Jeff and Ari just left to head to bed. Josh and Heather called it quits pretty much right after you dozed off."

"Why didn't you wake me up, Gunner?"

He shrugged. "You looked so peaceful sleeping with your head in my lap. I figured you needed the rest."

A part of me was disappointed Gunner would let me sleep. The idea was to spend time with our friends, but I knew I was being emotional and silly.

"You've only been asleep for maybe thirty or forty minutes."

Relief swept over my body. "Oh good! I thought maybe I had missed out on fun times."

Laughing, Gunner stood and reached for me. He took my hand and gently pulled me up to him.

"Well, after no one else showed interest in Ari's truth or dare game and we started talking about the ranch, you quickly dozed. Poor Heather's head was bopping all over the place before Josh got up and took her back to their tent."

Wrapping my arm around Gunner's waist, we slowly walked to our campsite. "Poor, Heather. I'm sure she is exhausted with carrying twins!"

"No doubt. I've never seen Josh so happy before. I mean, truly utterly happy."

Grinning, I held onto him tighter. "They're so perfect for each other."

Gunner stopped walking and turned to me. "Do you have any idea how much I love you?"

My nose crinkled up as I gazed into his eyes. "I think so, but maybe you should tell me."

He slowly grinned and replied, "I think I'd rather show you."

Eight

HEATHER

The moment I stepped out of the tent I was greeted with the smell of bacon. With my stomach voicing my hunger, I headed over to Jeff and Ari's campsite. Josh was manning the bacon while Jeff was at another stove tossing a pancake in the air.

The closer I got, the hungrier I became. Josh lifted his head and looked my way. My lower stomach pulled with desire. I had been so exhausted I fell asleep almost the moment my head hit the pillow last night. Josh held me against his body with his hand resting on the babies all night long.

"Hey, princess. How'd you sleep?" Josh asked while kissing me quickly on the lips.

"Better than I thought I would. I'm seriously surprised at how comfortable that blow-up mattress is."

Josh's face beamed. "I'm glad you slept good. I swear you were out before you even laid your head on the pillow."

"I'd imagine carrying around two little babies is exhausting," Jeff said with a wink and smile.

"I guess so. I wouldn't know what to compare it to, for me this seems like normal."

Ari walked over and sat down next to me. "I can't even imagine having more than one inside of me. This little one is pretty damn demanding on her own."

I rubbed my baby bump and smiled. I was showing a lot more than Ari, even though I was a few weeks behind her. "I'd have to say these two are for sure making their presence known in more than one way."

Wrapping her arm with mine, Ari gave me the warmest smile. "I'm so happy we're pregnant together."

I returned her smile. If someone would have told me a few years ago Ari and I would both be pregnant, and me with twins, I'd have laughed at them. We used to talk about how we were going to travel the world after college and explore places we dreamed of going to. Family and marriage was an afterthought. Now look at us. Both the happiest we'd ever been.

"Me too, Ari," I replied. "Even though I'm so much bigger than you."

She laughed. "You're carrying two of them. I've only got one."

Glancing over to the guys, I asked, "Do y'all need any help?"

Jeff and Josh both shook their heads. Jeff answered, "Nope. You two take it easy. Unlike Gunner, we've got our job of cooking down."

Ari moaned next to me. "Gunner. I really wanted to get him at truth or dare last night."

Josh whipped his head back and shot Ari a dirty look. "Then why did you pick me? You do know I'm fearing when it hits me."

The look on Ari's face was priceless. How she could pull off sweet and innocent was beyond me. In her best southern voice, she said, "Why, Josh Hayes, I declare I have *no idea* what you're talkin' 'bout."

He frowned then stated, "You will when you hear my screams of pain coming from the men's bathroom."

Ari lost it laughing, as did I. "That's disgusting, Hayes," Gunner said walking up with a jug of orange juice. My mouth started to water when he lifted it and grinned.

"How did you know I was craving orange juice?" I asked while standing and making my way over to him.

Gunner reached for a couple of plastic cups and poured two glasses, one for me and one for Ari.

"I remembered Ellie craving it and when I got up this morning for a run, I realized we didn't buy any last night. The park store had some though."

Ari downed her drink "I could kiss you right now, Gunner."

"Hey, hey, what's this?" Jeff asked as he set a giant plate full of pancakes on the table.

Ari and I both dug in, each taking four pancakes a piece.

"Wow, y'all are are eating a—"

Jeff stopped talking when both of our eyes swung up to glare at him.

"Um, I'll go make some more," Jeff said while giving Gunner a quick grin. "Hey, where's Ellie?"

I couldn't help but notice Gunner's face light up. "She's still sleeping. We were up late last night."

Jeff stopped walking and dropped his head. "Dude, really? I don't need that picture in my head."

Gunner flashed an evil smile at Ari and me and replied, "I didn't say anything."

"Josh! Are you trying to overcook the bacon?" Ari called out.

Glancing over his shoulder, Josh snarled his lip at Ari. "I swear, if you weren't married to my best friend."

Throwing out a light-hearted chuckle, Ari responded, "Please, you know you love me, assmole."

Josh walked over to the table and set two plates of bacon down. One in front of me, one in front of Ari. She reached across and took a few pieces. Taking a huge bite, she went to say something then stopped.

"What in the fuck is this rubber shit in my mouth?" Ari gasped.

Tasting the bacon, I shrugged. "Mine's good."

Ari leaned over and spit her bacon into her napkin. "Oh, God I'm going to hurl." She reached over and picked up a piece of the bacon. It was then I noticed it was shaped weird. Her eyes lifted slowly until she was giving Josh a death stare.

"What. Is. This?"

The boyish grin that appeared across Josh's face made me press my lips together to keep from laughing. "It's bacon, buttercup."

Tossing it back onto the plate, Ari shook her head. "No, Josh. What kind of bacon?"

Without missing a beat, he answered, "Soy."

Ari's tongue came out of her mouth as she attempted to wipe any remaining soy bacon from her mouth with her napkin.

"Gross! Oh, my gosh it's so gross!"

With a wink in my direction, Josh replied, "It's healthy. Didn't you say you wanted healthy?"

Ari glared at Josh. "No. I want pig bacon. Not soy or buffalo or almond!"

Josh pinched his brows? "Almond?"

Waving her hands about, Ari stood. "What the fuck ever! Almond milk, almond bacon, soy bacon. It's all healthy shit. I don't want healthy shit." She threw the soy bacon to Gus who sniffed then went and laid back over by Gunner.

"Even the dog doesn't want healthy crap," Ari stated.

"Actually, soy really isn't—"

When Ari turned to me, I stopped talking. I slid the plate of bacon her way. "I've got plenty of bacon."

Jeff glanced Josh's way and said, "You fucked up again, dude."

With a huff, Josh went back to cooking more bacon as Gunner and I both let out a soft chuckle.

———

Ellie and I walked arm in arm along the path while Gus followed close by. "How are you feeling?"

Smiling, I replied, "Amazing. The morning sickness still gets to me, but other than that, I feel really good."

"I can't imagine carrying two."

"What about you? How are you feeling?"

Her smile would have lit up a room, had we been inside one. "I feel wonderful. Alex is wonderful, Gunner is wonderful. It's all wonderful!"

I chuckled then let out a contented sigh. After everything Ellie had gone through with her father leaving them and her mother turning into an alcoholic, I was beyond thrilled to see her getting the happiness she deserved.

"So, the wedding," Ellie said as she looked at me.

"I don't want to talk about the wedding. Honestly, no stress this weekend. Let's just pretend like we have no responsibilities and have fun!"

Ellie laughed. "Done!"

Josh and Jeff were ahead of us arguing about something.

"What are those two going on about?" Ellie asked.

Ari walked up next to me and took my other arm with hers. "Something about who could climb up and back down that hill faster."

My mouth fell. "Are you serious? Why would they even want to? It's steep!"

With a chuckle, Ari nodded her head. "Yep. Gunner egged it on and is sitting back listening to the two of them argue about who is the tougher, stronger guy. I swear these men of ours. If I didn't love them all so much, I'd want to nut roll them."

Ellie and I both looked at Ari. "Nut roll them? What does that even mean?"

Ari's only response was an evil grin.

All three guys stopped while Josh and Jeff faced each other. Gunner picked up a stick and threw it for Gus who took off after it.

"Good lord. Why must everything be a competition between them?" Ellie pondered while we approached the two of them.

Jeff tossed his head back and let out a loud laugh. "Honestly, Josh. There is no way you can scale that hill."

"And you can, oh-mighty-one?" Josh spit back.

"Yes. Face it, you were raised in the city. You don't have what it takes to do things like this."

Josh jerked his head back. "You were raised in the city too, ass-hole."

Gunner laughed. "How about you both do it at the same time. First one up and back down can declare himself king of Garner State Park."

Walking over to Josh, I placed my hands on his chest. "This is silly, Josh. Let's move along and enjoy our hike."

He gave me the sweetest smile and kissed my forehead. "I love you, princess."

I breathed a sigh of relief.

"But I'm taking this dickhead down once and for all. I owe you for the whole Ford truck stunt."

My shoulders dropped as I stared at a very determined Josh.

Jeff was about on the ground laughing. "Damn. How you liking that truck, Josh? Got enough balls for ya?"

Josh let out some weird growl then placed his hands on my upper arms and looked into my eyes. "I need to do this."

I shook my head. "No. You really don't, Josh."

He smiled and kissed me quickly on the lips. "Thanks for under-standing, babe!" My eyes widened in shock as he walked over to the side of the hill with Jeff. They faced each other like they were about to enter a boxing ring.

"Oh hell … I have a feeling this isn't going to turn out so good," Ari said as she stood next to me.

My body shuddered as I watched Josh and Jeff race up the hillside. I held my breath when they started pushing each other out of the way.

"Same here," I whispered.

Nine

JOSH

Oh, he thinks he's gonna win? Hell no he isn't.

Jeff and I were neck and neck as we ran up the hill. Little did he know I'd been doing Crossfit classes for the last four months. My ass was in top shape.

"Fucking hell, Hayes!" Jeff called out as we raced to the top. With a wide grin, I knew I was going to at least beat him to the top. Knowing Jeff, he'd slide back down on his ass just to win.

I reached the top and pulled myself up. Lifting my hands above my head, I took in the moment to gloat at my victory. Jeff was almost to the top and I could tell he was struggling to make it.

"Steeper than it looks, isn't it?" I called out.

"Fuck you," he spat back while lifting himself over the edge.

Glancing down, Heather jumped and clapped. "Now be careful coming back down!" she called out.

Pesh, I had this. "I'm the king of the—"

Something crawled up my leg, causing me to look down. My eyes widened in horror as I let out a scream so loud I was sure my parents heard it in Austin.

"Get it off!" I yelled as I shook my leg. My foot slipped and I tumbled forward. Jeff reached out for me, but missed. The only thing I could do was hope and pray I didn't hit my head on one of the rocks on the way down. At the rate I was tumbling down the side of the hill, I was for sure going to win now.

Turning to Heather, I asked, "Are they out there?"

She attempted to hide her smile, but failed. "Yes."

I rolled my eyes. "Great. I'm never going to hear the end of this."

Heather shook her head. "Probably not. I'm just glad you're okay. You scared me to death when you slipped and came down that hill."

There was no denying Jeff would never let this go. Even my future wife and the mother of my kids was about to bust-out laughing.

Letting out a frustrated sigh, I motioned with my hands for her to let it out. "Just get it out now, will you."

She covered her mouth and lost it laughing. The nurse next to me chuckled as she finished wrapping my twisted ankle. Glancing up, she said, "At least you'll have a fun story to tell your kids."

Heather laughed harder.

"It's not that funny," I stated as I shot her a hardened stare.

Wiping away her tears, she nodded. "I know it's not. But it kind of is. I don't think I've ever heard you … heard you … you've never …"

She spun around and headed to the bathroom in the room. "Have … to … pee!"

I focused back on the nurse. It was clear she was laughing by the way her shoulders shook. "I don't like bugs."

Her eyes swung up to mine. "Are butterflies considered bugs?"

Another round of laughter came from the bathroom. The nurse chuckled and looked back at my ankle.

"You're very lucky you didn't break anything, Mr. Hayes. Or worse yet, hit your head on the way down."

Nodding, I replied, "I know. We're getting married in a couple of weeks. A broken anything wouldn't have been good." My chest puffed out. "But I won. That's all that matters."

She shook her head. "Uh-huh. So glad I never had boys."

After securing the wrap, she placed her hands on her hips and gave me a thoughtful smile. "No more trying to show off. And you'll want to keep off that ankle as much as possible. It's not a bad sprain, but it will be painful."

The door to the bathroom opened and Heather walked out, trying to keep from laughing. "Is he ready to go?" she asked the nurse.

"He is indeed. You'll want to stop at the Walgreens to get some Advil if you didn't bring any along."

Heather nodded. "Yes ma'am."

I looked at her in horror. "Wait. I'm not getting any pain pills? This thing is throbbing."

The nurse slowly turned to face me. Her left eye narrowed and for one brief moment, I felt the need to cover my junk.

"Mr. Hayes, you have a mild sprain of your ankle. You'll be fine with Advil and icing it."

"But—"

She lifted her hand. "Your future wife is going to give birth to two babies back to back. She's going to have to carry them for nine months. Two of them. Not one. Two." She lifted her hand and showed me two fingers.

I swallowed hard.

"I think Advil will take care of your *mild* sprain fine, just like the doctor said earlier."

With a fast nod, I replied, "Yes ma'am. I agree."

She handed me the papers and said, "You can check out at the front desk. Enjoy your camping trip."

Spinning on her heels, she headed out the door while Heather and I watched the door slowly shut.

Heather turned back to me and we both whispered, "Wow."

"I feel sorry for her husband when he gets sick," I said as I carefully got off the table. Heather chuckled and reached for my arm.

"Do you want the crutches?" she asked.

"Hell no. The second Jeff sees me with them it will be like an open invitation for him to start."

She pressed her lips together while looking at my ankle then back up at me. "Are you sure? They said to stay off of it."

"It's fine. It's only a *mild* sprain … remember?"

I went to take a step and nearly let out another girlish scream.

"Josh!" Heather gasped.

Reaching out, I stated, "Give me the damn crutches."

Without even attempting to hide her smile, Heather handed me the crutches.

I dragged in a deep breath and motioned for her to open the door. "It's stiff that's all. The quicker I get this over with … the better."

"It'll be fine. Everyone's glad you're not hurt. That's all that matters," Heather said as she walked next to me. The closer we got to the doors that lead to the waiting room, the more I dreaded my decision to run up that damn hill. Why did Jeff always try to one-up me?

Bastard.

Heather pushed the doors open and I maneuvered through them. I didn't see anyone in the waiting room and breathed a sigh of relief.

"They must have all gone back to the campsite," Heather stated.

"Good."

As we headed to the doors to leave, Heather asked, "Do you want to go home? I'm sure Gunner and Jeff wouldn't mind taking down our stuff."

I let out a gruff laugh. "There is no way I'm going home. Jeff would never let me live it down. I just need to take some Advil and I'll be fine."

We walked outside and Jeff was standing there with a giant bouquet of balloons. All of them were in a different shape and color of butterfly.

My mouth dropped open when he pulled out from behind his back a *My First Butterfly Collection* box.

"To help you get over your fear," he stated with a huge smile.

Lifting my crutch, I started after him as Heather cried out for me to stop.

Jeff laughed as he started to walk backwards while I hopped on one foot toward him.

I launched my weapon of choice, actually my only weapon, at him and he ducked. Unfortunately, Ari didn't.

Heather gasped when the crutch made contact.

My heart dropped as I whispered, "Oh. Shit."

Ari was covering her eye as she let out every curse word known to man. When she dropped her hand, I only saw evil coming from her one good eye.

Turning to Heather, I said, "Maybe we should go home … like now."

Ten

ARI

made my way out of our tent and headed to the table. Josh refused to make eye contact with me, which was probably a good thing.

"How's your eye, Ari?" Ellie asked.

Stopping directly in front of Josh, I smiled. "Good. You know what strikes me as funny?"

Josh glanced up at me and smiled. "What's that?"

I tilted my head and lifted my eyes up as if I was in deep thought before turning my attention back on him. "That you screamed like a scared little girl because you had a … butterfly … on your leg. And I get a crutch hurled at me and it strikes my eye, causing it to swell up and turn black, yet I didn't utter a peep."

Gunner lifted his hand and stated, "Um, I'd like to correct you on that, Ari. You did let out a rather scary sounding growl."

Josh's smile faded. "You know I'd have never have hit you with that crutch if your husband hadn't ducked like a pussy."

Jeff stood. "Hey, there is no need to bring that fact up!"

I shook my head. "You are both to blame and I know how you'll re-pay me."

Josh swallowed hard. "I don't like the sound of that."

With a sweet smile, I sat down next to Josh. "Don't get your panties into a twist, Hayes. I simply want furniture for the new baby's room."

"That's it?"

I lifted my brow. "I wouldn't think you're off the hook so easy. You haven't heard what I wanted yet."

"I am going to step in and say I have top priority in the making of baby furniture department," Heather stated with a chuckle.

"Totally agree with that," I replied.

Josh let out a fake laugh. "Okay, so I'm supposed to make the twins their furniture and now you want furniture?"

"Yep."

"You do know I have other jobs I have to do first … ones that pay me to make their furniture."

I nodded. "Of course, I don't want you to put anything on the back burner."

His brows pinched together. "Then how in the hell do you suggest I squeeze in your furniture?"

With a shrug, I replied, "That's not my problem, but I will say, Jeff here will be helping you."

"What?" Jeff asked as he glanced between Josh and me. "I can't make furniture."

With a wink, I stated, "Sure you can. Josh here just has to show you. Y'all will have to work *together* as a team."

Josh practically fell out of his chair. "I'm not teaching him how to make furniture! Have you ever tried to teach Jeff anything? He acts like he knows how to do it and doesn't even bother to listen."

"Hello, I'm sitting right here, and how hard could it possibly be to make furniture?"

Josh's mouth dropped open. "How hard could it be? Are you serious right now? You can't even mend a fence without bitching!"

I leaned back in my chair and folded my arms. A huge smile spread across my face.

Ellie giggled. "I totally see what you did there."

Gunner let out a roar of laughter. "Damn woman. Remind me never to get on your wrong side."

The canoes were all lined up along the shore while Jeff finished up paying.

"I love canoe rides!" Ellie stated with a huge smile.

I nudged her on the arm. "Wonder why?"

Her face lit up. It didn't seem like it was that long ago Gunner had whisked her away from her mother's house and took her out on the lake in a canoe. The memory of her telling me about their first kiss made me smile. We sure had all come a long way in a few short years.

"I don't think I'll ever forget that day," Ellie said as her cheeks heated.

Heather smiled. "It was the day Gunner kissed you for the first time, right?"

With a nod, Ellie replied, "Yep, sure was."

Gunner walked up and wrapped his arms around Ellie and kissed her on the cheek. "What are you girls all talking about with those smiles on your face?"

"The first time you ever kissed me down at Zilker Park."

Gunner's face lit up as he flashed that dimple of his. "Best day of my life."

Ellie turned and looked up at him. "Really?"

"Well, one of the best days of my life."

He leaned down and gently kissed her while Gus started barking. Gunner laughed and gave Gus a quick pat on the side and told him to get into the canoe, which he did. He gave Ellie one more kiss and gently ran his finger down her cheek.

A warmth spread over my body as I took in their love. Peeking over to Jeff, I watched as he and Josh argued about which way to go on the lake. I shook my head. *What is it with those two lately?*

I focused back on the kissing love birds. "All right, all right. Stop sucking face, you two. You're going to make me gag any second and we all know how weak my stomach is right now."

Heather pushed my arm as I turned to her and winked.

Jeff picked me up as I let out a small yelp. "Let me help you into the boat, babe."

With a quick kiss on the lips, I thanked him as he gently placed me in the canoe. Jeff turned to Josh and asked, "You need help getting in, Josh?"

Of course he ignored Jeff.

"Watch out there. I see a butterfly heading your way," Jeff called out. Josh simply lifted his hand and shot Jeff the finger.

"Stop teasing him about that," Ellie said as she lightly punched her brother on the arm. "It's bad enough he sprained his ankle."

Jeff tossed his head back. "He'll live. He's already walking around on it fine."

Ellie's hands went to her hips. "Why are the two of you going after each other so hard?"

With a shrug, Jeff replied, "I don't know. It's fun?"

Rolling her eyes, Ellie walked over to Gunner. He helped her into the canoe then pushed it into the lake and jumped in.

"Ready?" Jeff asked.

With a smile and nod, I replied, "Yep."

Pushing the canoe into the water, Jeff quickly jumped in. He glanced back and frowned. "Shit, I should have helped Josh."

My heart melted. No matter how much the two of them bickered and fought, they really were like brothers. I watched as Josh pushed the canoe into the water and barely threw himself into the canoe. Heather laughed as she helped him into the boat.

"I can't believe they are having twins," I said.

Jeff started rowing us further out as he peeked over his shoulder. "I think Josh is finally over the initial shock of it all. Now he's just nervous about the wedding. Then I think the whole twins thing will hit him again."

I chewed on my lip. "I can't imagine. I'm worried with having another one along with Luke! What would two the same age be like?"

With a light-hearted chuckle, Jeff shook his head. "Lots of sleepless nights that's for sure."

My eyes burned with the threat of tears.

Jeff reached out and took my hand. "Hey, what's wrong?"

"I'm not sure. What if things change?" I asked while I wiped a tear away.

His brows narrowed in. "What do you mean?"

"I don't know," I replied with a shrug. "Heather and Josh are going to be so busy with twins, we'll have another baby, before you know it Ellie and Gunner will be popping out another one. What if we all get so busy in our own worlds, we lose this?" I lifted my arms and motioned around me. "Time together as friends."

With a huge grin, he kissed the back of my hand. "Ari, we're still going to have that. It will just be with little ones running around."

Another tear slipped from my eye. "I don't want us to drift apart. I want our kids to grow up together and be the best of friends. I want to hear them argue like you and Josh do."

"They will, baby."

Chewing on my lip, I sighed. "Damn pregnancy emotions."

He laughed and started rowing again. "Jeff, promise me some day we'll be back here again. All of us, but this time it will be with our kids."

With a wink, he replied, "I'll do you one better. How about if we're here with our kids, and their kids."

My stomach fluttered. "I like that promise."

I watched as my husband's eyes filled with water. "So do I."

Eleven
JEFF

Glancing to my right, I couldn't help but smile as I watched Heather, Ellie, and Ari all sitting around the fire. Each of them had their noses buried in a book. Gus sat at their feet snoring away.

"It's nice seeing them relax, isn't it?" Gunner said.

I nodded. "Yeah. Hey, we need more firewood. Want to drive up to the store with me?"

"Sure. I'll let the girls know we're leaving."

I hit him on the back. "I'll see if Josh wants to go."

Gunner started toward the girls. "Sounds good. Meet you back at your truck."

As I made my way over to Josh, I couldn't but notice how deep in thought he was.

"Gunner and I are headed up to the park store for more wood. You want to come along?"

His head lifted as he answered, "Sure."

"What's that?" I asked, peeking over to something he was sketching out.

Sliding it my way, he answered, "Your baby's furniture."

I lifted the paper up and was blown away by what he had drawn. "Holy shit, this is amazing."

"Think Ari will like it?" Josh asked as he stood.

I lifted my eyes to his. "Dude, you know she was only kidding. She knows how busy you are."

"I know, but I feel really bad for hitting her in the eye."

My chest tightened as I glanced back at the drawing. "Are you being serious? You're really making this for us?"

"Yeah. Of course I am," he replied with a grin.

I'd never admit to anyone, especially Josh, but I was beyond moved by his gesture. "Dude, this is incredible. Ari's going to flip."

"So you think she'll be happy with it?"

I looked back at the design. "Josh, I'm kind of at a loss for words right now."

"Well hell, let me snap shot this moment into my memory. Jeff at a loss of words."

Laughing, I glanced back at him. "Ha ha. Seriously though, this is amazing."

"The crib will be the same design regardless if it's a boy or a girl, I'll just adjust the canopy and a few things when you find out the sex. I have to tell ya, I have a crazy feeling it's a girl."

My heart raced. I reached out and pulled Josh in and gave him a bro hug. Hitting him hard on the back, I said, "Thanks, dude. For everything."

Josh hit me back … harder. "Always, Jeff."

"For Christ's sake. I leave you two alone for five minutes and I walk up on y'all hugging on each other? What in the hell is that about?"

I pushed Josh back lightly. "Josh is trying to pull on my heart strings by getting to me through my unborn child."

Gunner walked up and I handed him the drawing. "Damn, Josh. It's beautiful."

"Thanks. I appreciate that," Josh answered with a proud grin.

"Hell, if this is what you have for Ari, I can't imagine what you have planned for the twins."

Josh beamed with happiness. "My dad's helping me with it, but I think Heather is going to love it."

"If you made it, you know she will. It makes it all the more special," Gunner said as he handed Josh the paper.

I clapped my hands together. "Let's head on up and get us some wood."

"Ellie asked for S'mores fixins and they mentioned going to the dance up at the pavilion."

Spinning Ari, I pulled her back against my body as we slid across the dance floor to a George Strait song.

Her smile alone told me she was having a blast.

When the song ended, she let out a laugh and said, "I'm exhausted! Can we sit for a bit?"

"Of course we can," I said as I wrapped my arm around her waist and guided her over to our table.

"Taking a break?" Ellie asked.

"Whew! Yes, man we were cutting a rug I tell ya," Ari said as she took a seat and downed almost a whole bottle of water.

Glancing over to Josh and Heather, I asked, "Y'all not dancing tonight?"

Josh and Heather laughed as Josh said, "Dude, we were just out there dancing."

Placing her hand over her heart, Heather sighed. "Goes to show you how in love the two of you still are. You only see each other."

My eyes locked with Ari's. The flutter in my chest was something I would never grow tired of. "I am for sure madly in love with this one."

A sweet smile spread across Ari's face before she glanced around the table. "I don't know about the rest of you, but I'm ready to head back and snuggle up by a fire."

Ellie jumped up. "Yes! S'mores time!"

The sound of the fire cracking was peaceful as I leaned back and sighed. "I'm never eating another S'more again for the rest of my life."

"I'm going to agree with you on that one," Ari said covering her mouth. "I feel like I'm going to hurl."

Ellie giggled. "Stop being so dramatic, you two. You didn't eat nearly as many as I did."

Ari moaned. "I know, Ells. Just watching you eat them made me feel sick. I'm ready to head back to our tent."

My dick jumped at the idea of finally being alone with Ari.

Throwing her a wink, I said, "I think heading back to the tent is a great idea."

"No! You can't go to sleep now! Who's up for a midnight hike?" Ellie cried out.

Everyone turned to Ellie. "Are you crazy?" Heather asked. "I'm barely keeping my eyes open. I'm exhausted."

With a pout, Ellie folded her arms across her chest. "Seriously? Is everyone going to call it a night?"

Drawing Ari in close to me, I wiggled my brows and said, "I didn't say we were calling it a night. I simply said I thought heading to the tent was a good idea."

Covering her mouth, Ellie pretended to gag. "Gross."

Heather sighed as she stood. "I'm sorry, Ells. I really am tired and I don't think a hike is a great idea for Josh. He's been on his ankle all day."

Ellie let out a frustrated groan. "Fine. Be party poopers."

Gunner reached for Ellie's hand. "They're both pregnant, sweetheart. I'm sure they're tired. We've had a busy day."

"Hike in the morning?" Ellie asked with a hopeful voice.

Ari and I stood as Ari answered, "Yeah, I wouldn't hold your breath on that one either."

I took Ari's hand in mine. "Goodnight, y'all. Stay warm, it's getting down to the upper forties tonight."

"We're right behind ya," Josh said as he helped Heather up and wrapped his arm around her.

After all the goodnights, Ari and I made it back to the tent. I wiggled my brows and started to strip.

"As much as I would love to be together … I'm exhausted, Jeff. All that dancing tonight did me in."

Disappointment rushed through my body, but I wouldn't let her see it. I knew she was tired and hadn't been feeling good with her morning sickness that really lasted all day and night.

"I'm good just snuggling up to you, baby."

With a grin, she quickly stripped out of her clothes and climbed onto the air mattress.

"Does it need filling up? I filled it up before we headed out to the fire."

She snuggled under the covers. "Nope. Feels great."

I slipped in next to her and pulled her body against mine. "Feels like someone thinks he's gonna get lucky after all."

My lips peppered her back with soft kisses as she let out a soft moan. I let my hands explore her body. Ari lifted her leg, silently begging me to touch her.

"Thought you were tired," I whispered against her ear.

"A girl can change her mind, can't she?"

My heartbeat increased as I moved my hand into position, ready to feel how much she wanted me.

That's when it happened.

Everything that was good and amazing about the moment changed when Ari let out the longest, loudest, fart known to the history of man.

I jumped out from the covers and plugged my nose.

"What in the hell was that?"

Ari turned to face me, a slightly evil smile on her face. "I think I ate too much hummus maybe? I have gas."

The smell swept around my body and somehow managed to get into my nose … even though I was squeezing it shut with my fingers.

Gagging, I shook my head and dropped my hands. "No shit! Damn, Ari. You ruined the mood."

"I'm tired anyway, it's safe to come back in."

She patted the bed and tried to hide her smile.

I crawled in and fluffed out the covers. "I swear, if I didn't love you so much and you weren't pregnant with my child, I may have to re-think things."

Rolling her eyes, Ari sighed. "Please, like you've never farted before."

"Not like that! I'm pretty sure the earth shook some."

With a giggle, she pulled my arm over her. "I love you, Jeff."

Drawing her body closer to mine, I smiled. "I love you too." My hand rubbed across her swollen stomach. "Goodnight, sweet baby."

It didn't take long before the sounds of Ari's breathing lulled me to sleep. The peacefulness didn't last long. I felt like I'd only just fallen asleep when Ari woke me up again.

"Jeff! Jeff wake up!"

Ari was rocking my body with one hand, while poking my back with her finger.

"I thought you were tired."

She poked me again. "Jeff! There's something outside the tent. I think it's a bear!"

With a chuckle, I laughed. "There are no bears here."

A loud crash caused me to sit up.

"Told you. It sounds like it's trying to get into the food."

More rustling came from outside as I sighed. "Damn raccoons."

Quickly getting up, I started to unzip the tent.

"Wait!" Ari whispered. "You're naked."

Staring at her, I shook my head. "So? I seriously doubt the raccoon is going to care."

"Well, what if someone sees you?"

"Someone like who? The raccoon?"

Rolling her eyes, she waved me off. "Fine, go out there naked then. If Ellie sees you, you'll be scarred for life."

"It's three in the morning, baby. I seriously doubt anyone, let alone Ellie, is out."

I finished unzipping the tent and jumped out with my hands flailing in the air.

"Rawr! Get! Boo! YaYa! Scat on out of here you …"

My eyes were drawn to the creature on the picnic table. Our eyes met and I knew the moment the skunk turned around, I was screwed.

"Oh, son-of-a-bitch no!" I cried out as I was about to run back into the tent. The second the spray hit me, I started screaming like a little girl. It was too late. My entire front half was covered.

"Jeff!"

Ari rushed out of the tent and started gagging.

"Oh no," she cried out while covering her mouth and nose.

I nodded and shrugged. "Well, it wasn't a raccoon."

Her shoulders sunk and even in the moonlight I could see the look on her face before she rolled eyes.

Twelve

GUNNER

W arm breath kissed the back of my neck. "Hmm."

"Gunner? Did you hear someone scream?"

Rolling over, I came face to face with my beautiful wife. "No. I didn't hear anything."

A small patch of moonlight peeked in through the tent, lighting Ellie's face enough to show her frowning.

"I swear I heard someone yelling, then scream. It sounded like a girl."

With a frown, I shook my head. "I didn't hear anything."

Ellie leaned in closer, her lips inches from mine. "Maybe I was dreaming of Josh falling again. I'm sorry I woke you up."

Lifting my hand, I placed it on the side of her soft cheek. "I'm not."

Her teeth sunk into her lip as she leaned into my touch. With a soft, sweet voice, she whispered my name. "Gunner."

My hand slipped behind her neck, drawing her mouth to mine. Her kisses were like crack. I couldn't get enough of them. Enough of her.

Ellie rolled to her back while I pressed against her entrance. What started out as a sweet kiss turned into something needier. Our hands explored every inch of each other. I rolled each nipple between my fingers, causing her to arch her back and let out a soft moan each time.

"Yes," she hissed through her teeth.

Pulling back from our kiss, I whispered against her lips, "You're so beautiful, sweetheart."

"Make love to me, Drew. Please." My heart nearly stopped each time Ellie whispered my real name.

Slipping my other hand between her legs, I felt her desire for me.

"Jesus, Ells. Always so ready for me."

Her head thrashed back and forth as I slowly slid inch by inch inside of her. When she couldn't take it anymore, she wrapped her legs around me and drew me deep inside. Each in and out motion sent me closer to my edge. Little moans of pleasure slipped from Ellie's mouth as she met me thrust for thrust. A slight sheen moved across our bodies as we both reached our climax together.

"Gunner!" Ellie cried out as I pressed my mouth to hers. Swallowing her moans of pleasure.

Heat coursed through my body, even as I stilled. I didn't want to leave behind the feeling of being inside of her.

"I love you, Ellie."

A single tear slipped from her eye. Reaching down, I kissed it away.

"I love you more, Drew."

Reaching over, I grabbed a shirt from the tent floor. I pulled out of her and quickly wiped myself and then tended to Ellie.

After stowing the T-shirt to the side of the tent, I drew Ellie's body in closer to mine.

With my arms wrapped tightly around the love of my life, I kissed her shoulder then spoke. "I've never felt so alive. It's like every time we're together, I fall more in love with you."

Turning in my arms, Ellie's nose practically touched my own. My mind drifted back to that first day I met Ellie. Sitting in Jeff's truck, anxious as hell to meet the little sister who was off limits. I couldn't help but smile.

"I feel the same way. My heart feels like it will explode with every touch and kiss you give me. Your love fills me completely."

Ellie's eyes soon grew heavy. I watched as she finally let them close and drifted to sleep. This woman was my entire life. There wasn't anything I wouldn't do for her. When I couldn't keep my own eyes open, I let my body relax and slipped into a deep sleep. Dreaming of the very woman I held in my arms.

Unzipping the tent, I stepped out and then turned to help Ellie.

"Man it's chilly out here!" Ellie gasped.

I pulled a sweatshirt over my long-sleeved shirt and handed one to her. She slipped it on and then placed a hat over her head.

Ellie looked around me and frowned. "What in the world is Jeff doing?" Glancing over my shoulder, I noticed he was sitting in what looked like a metal tub.

"No idea. Let's go see."

Taking her hand, we made our way over to Jeff and Ari's campsite. The closer we got, the clearer it became.

"Um, I think I know what that scream was you heard last night."

Ellie pinched her nose together. "Lord have mercy, there's a skunk somewhere!"

A few steps closer and Ellie got it.

"Oh no, Jeff. You got hit with a skunk?"

Jeff was sitting in a tub of tomatoes. Ari sat on top of the picnic table and grinned from ear to ear while eating an apple.

Peering into the tub, I jumped back. "Dude, are you naked?"

"Fuck yes, I'm naked. I've been sprayed by a skunk!"

I rubbed my eyes. "A warning would be appreciated next time."

"Why are you in tomatoes?" Ellie asked.

"Thank you, Ellie," Ari stated as she glared over at Jeff.

He rolled his eyes. "It takes the skunk smell away."

With a chuckle, I shook my head. "Dude, no it doesn't."

Jeff's eyes widened. "What do you mean it doesn't? Yes. It does." He frowned and then asked, "Doesn't it?"

Ellie laughed. "You need to mix peroxide, baking soda, and liquid detergent together. That's what you use."

"It's not tomatoes?"

Now it was my turn to laugh. "No, who told you that?"

Jeff's face turned the color of the tomatoes. "Josh! He came over last night after I got sprayed to see if everything was okay. He was the one who told me to get canned tomatoes and soak in them."

I rubbed the back of my neck and sighed. "Dude, that's only going to mask the smell. You need to get it off of you."

Jeff stood. Butt-ass naked with tomatoes dripping off his body. His … whole … body.

"Oh, my God my eyes!" Ellie screamed as she spun around. "It hurts! It hurts so bad!"

Balling his fists, Jeff slowly spoke. "I'm … going … to … kill … him."

I tired like hell to cover my laugh, but the second Josh walked up and said good morning and Jeff went after him, I lost it.

"Jesus, Mary, and Joseph! Jeff really? There are kids at this park!" Ari called out as Jeff chased Josh around the three campsites. She turned to me and Ellie and sighed. "I tried telling him last night, but he wouldn't listen. Do you know how bad he is going to stink up my house? He may have to sleep in the barn."

Heather approached us. She looked at Jeff and Josh, then back to us. "Do I want to know?" she asked.

Ari and Ellie both responded. "Nope."

With a shrug, she walked over to the cooler, opened it and asked, "What's for breakfast?"

ELLIE

The sound of the wind blowing lightly through the trees had me dropping my head back and smiling.

"Aren't you supposed to be painting, Ells?" Ari asked in a hushed voice.

"I'm enjoying the sounds of nature and the peeks of sun through the threes on my face. Let me have this moment. Plus, my hand is cramping."

Ari chuckled. "Don't let the teacher see you. She already yelled at that poor old lady for closing her eyes and humming.

Focusing back on the work in front of me, I stared at it.

With a grimaced face, I stated, "Mine doesn't look like it's supposed to."

Peeking over at mine, Heather chuckled. "Looks better than mine."

I glanced at hers and we both started laughing.

"Ladies in the back, did you need some help?"

Instantly, I felt my cheeks heat as Heather and I shook our heads.

"This class is for serious painters, ladies. Unless you can zip it, you'll be asked to take your canvas and vacate."

Heather picked up her brush and fumbled over her words. "Yes, sir … I mean ma'am. Yes, ma'am."

After a few seconds, Ari leaned over, "You totally just got schooled by the instructor."

Pushing her away, I put my finger to my mouth for her to hush up.

"Okay, is she serious? For serious painters? It was an open class put on by the park!"

Aril shrugged. "I guess she takes it serious."

I dragged in a deep breath and focused back in on my painting. Tilting my head, I stared at it. With a quick peek at Ari's, I groaned internally. Her painting was perfect. The mason jar was spot-on and the flowers she had put in it were beautiful. The colors reminded me of the west pasture during this time of year. The flowers in full bloom. I could almost smell them.

Then you had my drawing. I turned back to it. My jar looked like a paint can. The flowers were basically sticks coming out of the can with weeds sprouting out.

Then I saw it.

Holy crap. Are you kidding me?

At the bottom of the painting we were to paint the words *Wild Flowers.* Mine read, *Mild Flowers. How in the hell did I do that?*

I covered my mouth to hold back my laughter.

"What's so funny?" Heather asked.

When I looked back at her tic-tac-toe painting I couldn't hold it in, even though I tried like hell to. My strained laugh came out sounding like someone dragging a metal chair across the floor.

The instructor didn't look my way. Clearly she was too involved with the painter in the very front who was probably knocking it out of the park with their painting.

I covered my mouth with both hands as I pointed to Heather's painting.

"Are you playing against yourself?" I asked.

Heather shook her head and pointed to the girl who was sitting on the other side of her. "Alison's playing."

Leaning back, I waved to Alison. When I looked at her painting, I chuckled again. It was a giant blob of blue with yellow dots.

"What is going on with y'all? She's going to yell at you again, Ellie," Ari stated with a stern expression.

I pointed to where I had painted *Mild* instead of *Wild*. It didn't take long for the four of us to get the giggles. The more we tried to hide it, the worse it became. The next thing I knew, the instructor was standing in front of us, hands on her hips and one pissed off look on her face.

"May I ask what is so amusing?"

It was right about then Gunner and Jeff walked up. "Hello ladies, how's the painting coming?"

The instructor rolled her eyes and spun around, her pointer finger ready to start pointing as she yelled at them for interrupting the Zen of the painting. She jumped back and covered her nose.

"Excuse me, you are interrupting my class, and that smell!"

Jeff shrugged and smiled. "Skunk attack at two in the morning."

The instructor gagged then turned to Gunner. "Oh, well hello there. Are you um, are you interested in painting?"

Gunner flashed that melt-your-panties smile of his at her. "No ma'am. I'm sorry we interrupted. I thought the class would be over by now."

The instructor playfully swatted at Gunner as her cheeks blushed. "You're not interrupted at all! Not. At. All."

My mouth fell as I gave her a dazed look.

Ari reached over and placed her finger on my chin, lifting it until my lips met. "You're going to catch flies, Ellie."

Swinging my gaze to Ari, I shook my head. "Do you see this right now?"

Ari chuckled. "I see it."

Jeff stepped forward and tipped his hat at our art teacher and made his way over to Ari. She quickly stepped to the side and tried to wave the smell away. Leaning down, he kissed her softly on the lips, eliciting sighs from all the women in the area.

"Wow, look at your painting. Where will we hang it?" Jeff asked.

Ari wore a huge grin. "The baby's room."

Awe's were heard across the lawn. Even with Jeff stinking like high hell, his good looks still drew the ladies in.

When I looked back at Gunner, our instructor was still eyeing him like she was ready to pounce on him. I cleared my throat, drawing Gunner's attention over to me. His smile came to life, filling my chest with warmth.

Oh, how I loved this man.

"Excuse me ma'am, but my beautiful wife is right there."

"He's good," Heather whispered as she started to clean up her painting area. Her and Alison quickly got lost in a conversation.

"Hey there, sweetheart. How was the painting class?"

I shrugged. "I'm pretty sure folks won't be lining up to buy my work anytime soon."

Gunner pulled me to him and hugged me. "Nonsense. That is a priceless piece of work. Look at how beautiful and ... unique it is."

My arms instinctively wrapped around his body. "I love you, but you are a terrible liar, Gunner Mathews."

"What? I'm not lying."

"It's unique all right," Ari threw in. "She was supposed to put wild flowers, and she put mild."

Gunner tilted his head and stared at the painting. "Wait. Is that a mason jar or a can of paint?"

Playfully pushing him away, my hands went to my hips. "Ugh. I hate painting."

The instructor tsked. "Don't blame the canvas for the brush not working."

I rolled my eyes and finished cleaning up. Gunner and Jeff took our paintings and we headed back to the campsite. It was hard walking near

Jeff; he still smelled like skunk. I wasn't sure how Ari was going to sleep in the tent with him tonight.

"Jeff, did you soak in the mixture?" I asked while waving my hand in front of my nose.

Ari giggled and glanced back over her shoulder at Heather who was walking with Alison.

"I did soak in it … twice. Apparently you need to do it almost immediately. Hopefully a few more soaks and the smell will be off of me."

Gunner chuckled. "Only you would get sprayed by a skunk."

With a groan, Jeff responded, "Tell me about it."

Heather walked up alongside of me. "Hey, where is your painting?" I asked.

"I left it there! I just did the class for fun 'cause you and Ari wanted to do it."

I looked around. "Where did Alison go?"

"She headed back to her campsite to get lunch ready for her husband. He's been fishing while she took the art class. I may head over to her campsite to chat for a bit later. Introduce Josh to her and her husband."

My heart dropped. "Really? But, you don't even know her."

Heather shrugged. "I know, she seems really nice though. She's a kindergarten teacher, and I think Josh will get along with her husband. He loves working with wood. Plus, they live outside of Fredericksburg. How cool is that?"

I forced a fake smile. "Pretty cool. Hey, I thought we were all going to go for that hike?"

"I don't think it's such a great idea with Josh's ankle. Besides, I'm not really feeling up for a long hike, Ells."

"It doesn't have to be long."

Heather gave me a sweet smile. "Still not feeling it. You and Gunner should go, spend some time together. I'm sure Jeff and Ari wouldn't mind some alone time as well."

With a nod, I replied, "Yeah. Sounds good."

I had no idea why I was feeling the way I was. It was nothing but jealousy and downright childish. I knew it was wrong to be upset with her, but I was. As she talked to Ari about this Alison girl, I grew more and more upset. This was *our* friends camping trip and she was leaving us to go spend time with some strange woman.

"So, what's on the agenda for this afternoon?" Jeff asked.

Everyone looked at me. "Heather has already made plans, so everyone just figure out what you want to do. I couldn't care less."

I spun on my heels and practically stomped off.

Trying like hell to stop the tears from falling, I took in a deep breath and blew it out.

I would regret my silly behavior later, but for now I needed to get away from everyone and clear my head.

Fourteen

ARI

"What in the hell was that all about?" I asked while we all watched Ellie walk off with a serious pout on her face.

"You don't think she's upset about Alison, do you?" Heather asked.

Gunner walked up next to me, his eyes still on his retreating wife. "Who's Alison?"

"Heather was sitting next to her in that stupid art class," I said. Glancing over to Heather, I narrowed my brows. "What did you say to her?"

Her eyes widened in shock. "Me? Why do you think it was me who upset her?"

I shrugged. "Oh, I don't know. Maybe because she was fine until you talked to her. Then she got all weird. I mean, what was with the whole thing about *Heather already has plans*?"

"I simply said I didn't want to go on a hike and that Josh and I were going to go over to Alison and her husband's campsite. Then I suggested that her and Gunner spend some time together. I might have also said y'all would probably like to spend some alone time with each other."

I gasped. "Wh-what?"

"What?" Heather asked while swinging her eyes between the three of us.

Jeff held up his hands. "I'm staying out of this one. Totally neutral."

Gunner stuck his hands in his pockets and locked his lips shut.

Turning back to Heather, I glared at her. "I can't believe you made plans with another couple on our couples camping trip!"

"Are you serious right now, Ari?"

"Yes! You might as well have told Ellie you're tired of hanging out with her and you're going to find someone knew to hang with."

Heather threw her hands up in the air and huffed. "This is insane. Are we not allowed to have friends outside of this group?"

"Of course we are, but we're on this trip together. You know how much Ellie's been wanting to go on a hike. You blew her off for this ... Alison chick. Who, to be honest with you, was looking a little too hard at Gunner, if you ask me."

"Me?" Gunner asked all innocent and cute. "Why are you dragging me into this?"

"Because she was. She was eye fucking you more than the art instructor was."

"That's insane!" Heather said with a gruff laugh. "We were talking the entire time and she seems nice."

My eyes met Heather's. "I know what I saw, Heather. My bet is this girl is trying to get in with the group."

"What? Yes, she mentioned possibly coming over this evening and hanging out around the fire, but that was it. Maybe they just want to meet new friends. Why are you being so weird about this?"

"When did she invite y'all over? Before or after Gunner showed up?"

Heather shook her head and folded her arms across her chest. "I'm not doing this with you. Ellie is behaving like a child who is not getting her way and honestly I'm a little surprised by her behavior. I don't want to go on some stupid hike! I didn't even want to come on this damn camping trip in the first place!"

"Gunner? We … um … we need to run up to the park store."

All eyes turned to see Ellie standing there. Her eyes were filled with tears, and I instantly started to walk her way. She held up her hand and forced a smile.

"I'm sorry if y'all are not having fun. Jeff and I thought this would be a fun way to spend the weekend, but I understand if you're not enjoying yourselves. If you want to leave, I understand."

Heather walked up next to me, "Ellie—"

With her chin trembling, Ellie forced a smile. "It's fine, Heather. Go hang out with Alison and her husband. I'm sure they're nice people. And honestly, if you'd feel better leaving, that's totally fine. I'm sorry for my … childish behavior."

Spinning on her heels, Ellie quickly walked over to Gunner's truck.

Anger filled my body instantly as I looked at Heather. "Well, looks like you just got your free ticket to go home."

"Wait, Ari, that's not fair. You didn't want to come on this camping trip either!"

"I'm actually enjoying myself, Heather, if you haven't noticed. I miss Luke like mad, but being all together has been exactly what I needed. I'm sorry if you don't feel the same way." I shook my head in disgust. "And I would never say something to hurt Ellie. Never."

Heather's mouth dropped open. "I didn't know she was there or I would never have said anything! This is so stupid. I didn't realize we were still in high school and couldn't have friends outside our circle."

I slowly shook my head. "You don't get it, do you? The whole reason Ellie wanted to do this trip was because she's worried we're all going to drift apart, and to be honest, I feel the same way. Maybe it's time we did drift apart some."

Heather's chin trembled and her eyes filled with tears. I hated to admit it, but I wanted her to hurt as much as she had hurt Ellie.

"What are you saying, Ari?"

Jeff walked up to me and turned me to him. "Hey, I think both of y'all are feeling overly emotional. Let's call a truce, we can talk to Ellie, Heather can go hang with this couple and everything will be okay. We'll all meet up later."

Turning to look at Heather, I swung my eyes back to Jeff. "Fine. I'm afraid I'm about to say something I'll regret anyway."

As I started back to our campsite, Heather called out my name. "Ari. Ari, wait. Ari, come on, please wait!"

I kept walking, my eyes fixed on my best friend sitting in Gunner's truck. She looked out the window with an empty stare.

"Hey, you want to talk to her?" Gunner asked.

Chewing on my lip, I walked over to the truck and tapped on the window. Ellie looked up and opened the door.

"You okay?" I asked with a smile.

Ellie sniffled and wiped her nose as she got out of the truck.

"I'm being silly and acting like a child. I don't know why. Maybe it's the baby blues setting in late, or knowing all of this is going to be changing soon. I don't know. Maybe it's me being a mother has me thinking of my own mother. I don't know, but I'm sorry."

I reached for her hand and squeezed it. "No, you're not acting like a child. Heather is being Heather. If she wants to hang out with this girl, let her."

Ellie shrugged. "I'm scared, Ari. I'm scared this is going to be the last time we all hang out like this. After the babies come, we're never going to have time to do anything. I'd be lost without y'all."

The corner of my mouth rose some as I shook my head. "We are so much alike, Ellie Mathews. I was telling your brother the same exact thing, and guess what?"

"What?" she asked.

"It's not true. We've been friends a long time."

She chuckled and wiped a tear away. "Yeah, we have."

"Nothing is ever going to change that. We're going to have to work harder at finding time to do things like this though."

"I know. I have no idea why I got so emotional."

My brows lifted as hope filled my body. "Pregnant?"

"No," she replied with a chuckle. "Like I said, maybe it's some post-post-post baby blues."

I nodded. "Maybe. Are you feeling better though?"

Her face lit up with a smile. "Yes, thank you, Ari. You always did know how to cheer me up."

I shrugged then laughed. "Hey, do you remember the time I talked you into skipping school and we went to Zilker Park?"

Covering her hand with her mouth, Ellie chuckled. "Yes! And we fell asleep and got so sunburnt!"

"The next day at school the principal asked what happened to us."

We both started laughing. "And you told him it was a chemistry experiment gone wrong!"

"Yes!" I cried out as our laughter quickly grew. "I said it blew up and burned our faces!"

With a snort and laugh, Ellie added, "And he sent us to the nurse who told us we were both going to hell for lying because we were clearly sunburnt!"

Ellie and I were laughing so hard, I had tears streaming down my face.

"I take it you're both feeling better?" Gunner asked while walking up to us.

Once we were able to get ourselves under control, Ellie nodded. "Thanks, Ari. I'm sorry I was acting like a child.

"You weren't, so don't even think twice about it."

We hugged and both whispered we loved each other. Pushing back, I grinned. "So why don't you and Gunner head to the store, then we'll head out on that hike."

Her face lit up. "Sounds good."

Jeff and I walked hand in hand over to Gunner and Ellie's campsite. When I saw Heather, Josh, Alison, and another guy walking up, I started to say something, but Jeff squeezed my hand.

"Play nice, Arianna."

I groaned slightly.

"Ari, Jeff, you remember Alison."

We both nodded as Heather pointed to the guy standing next to her. "This is Alison's husband, Grant."

Looking the guy over, I smiled slightly. He was tall, slightly built and wasn't bad looking. The baseball cap he wore hid the color of his hair.

Jeff reached out and shook his hand and said, "Nice to meet you, Grant."

"My pleasure," Grant answered with a wide grin on his face. He turned and looked at me. The way his eyes raked over my body made my skin crawl. "And you must be Ari. Heather's told us you're expecting as well. We've never done this with pregnant women, but it should be fun."

The fake ass smile on my face faded. Frowning, I asked, "What could be fun?"

Alison giggled and said, "Ignore him, Ari."

Jeff and I looked at each other. He leaned down and whispered against my ear, "Are you getting a weird vibe, or is it just me?"

"Nope, I've got it too."

Jeff glanced back over to Heather and the couple. "What brings y'all over here?" Jeff asked.

Heather frowned slightly. "Well, I mentioned that everyone was going on a hike."

"You mean *we* were going on a hike and you were sitting it out?" I asked with a smirk.

"Yes, Ari," Heather said with a smile.

"Alison and Grant thought it would be a fun to go and get a chance to meet y'all. She was um … eager for her husband to meet … ah … Gunner and Ellie."

My eyes fixed in on Alison. Her smile was a little too big and a little too eager. "Huh. Well, we were heading over to get them now."

"No need, we saw y'all making your way over," Gunner said as he and Ellie walked up.

"Gunner. It's so great seeing you again," Alison said as she reached her hand out for him. And not a hand shake reach, but a *kiss the back of my hand because I'm a fucking princess* reach.

He glanced down at it and simply gave her a head pop.

Heather cleared her throat and said, "Gunner, Ellie, this is Grant, Alison's husband."

Grant reached his hand out to shake Gunner's then took Ellie's hand and kissed the back of it. "What beautiful eyes you have, Ellie. The way they compete with the sky is amazing. Breathtaking."

Oh. My. God. He did *not* just flirt with her out in the open like that.

"Um … thank you?" Ellie replied, making it sound like a question. I couldn't help but notice how Gunner looked like he was ready to pounce on Grant.

I turned back to Alison to see her reaction and she stood there with a smile. Heather on the other hand looked shocked as hell. *I wonder if it is too soon to say I told you so?*

"All right. Are we ready to get this party started?" Josh asked.

"Hell yes. This is going to be one hell of an adventure, right baby?" Grant said as he grabbed Alison's ass and they started walking.

Jeff and I stayed back with Gunner and Ellie.

Taking a few steps forward, Jeff turned to us. "Anyone else get the feeling we need to walk in the opposite direction of them?"

"What in the hell was that?" Gunner asked with a dumbfounded expression.

"Did he flirt with me? Like seriously right there in front of his wife?" Ellie asked.

"Yeah, well at least he didn't eye fuck the hell out of you like he did Ari," Jeff replied.

I shook my head. "Y'all ... I've got a weird feeling about these two."

Gunner took Ellie's hand. "I think maybe we're all overreacting here. Let's go on the hike, make the best of Heather bringing her new friends along, and enjoy the time together."

Heather had stopped and called back. "Are y'all coming?"

"Yep!" Ellie exclaimed as the four of us reluctantly started walking toward the trailhead.

Fifteen

HEATHER

I slowed my pace down and walked next to Josh as the others pulled slightly ahead. He said his ankle was feeling better, but I knew by his slowing pace, it was bothering him. "Okay, so I might have been wrong about something."

Josh grinned. "About what? Ellie doesn't seem to be angry and neither does Ari."

"No, it's nothing about what happened between us. It's not the first time we've gotten into a tiff."

Josh gave me an inquisitive look. "Then what were you wrong about?"

"Ari mentioned Alison looking at Gunner like she was interested in him. I told her she was crazy, but the way Alison reacted when Gunner walked up, and now she keeps slightly touching him every time she talks to him. I think Ari was right. Alison has the hots for Gunner!"

Josh chuckled. "Heather, come on. The girl seems really friendly. Didn't you notice how she was doing the same thing to me? I thought it was kind of strange how openly she flirted with me, but I think that's just her. She's doing it with Jeff as well, and Grant doesn't seem to mind."

A sick feeling settled in the pit of my stomach. I had noticed how she was flirting with Josh and it immediately bothered me. When I mentioned us having to leave to go on a hike, I was stunned they invited themselves to come along. "That's the other thing, Josh. Grant made an off-the-wall comment about Ari being pregnant and how this would be a new adventure. I was thinking he meant the hike, but why would going on a hike with two pregnant women be an adventure? If anything, it would be trying if they were to slow him down. Then when he flirted with Ellie, I thought Gunner was going to grab Grant and throw him to the ground."

"What did he say? How did I miss that?" Josh asked.

I chewed on lip. Something wasn't right. "You were messing with Gus and didn't hear him. He told her how beautiful her eyes were. That they were breathtaking or something like that and he kissed the back of her hand."

Rolling his eyes, Josh started walking. "Okay, it sounds to me like the both of them are just really open talkers. They say what's on their minds. Maybe innocent flirting doesn't bother them any."

Even as I attempted to push the strange vibes away, they grew larger. I watched as Gus kept running up to Grant and barking at him. Gunner finally put Gus on a leash and kept him away from Grant.

Even the dog got a weird vibe.

Grant pointed ahead. "Alison and I come here a lot; we've used the trail up ahead before. There are even a few benches we can use to make things more comfortable."

Ari sighed. "I could really use a few minutes to sit."

Grant stopped and took Ari's hand. "And I know exactly what you can sit on."

Pulling her hand out of his, Ari's face turned white. Grant gave her a wink and started walking.

Josh and I came to a stop next to Ari.

"Did he just? I mean … was he talking about the bench or was he talking about …"

Josh turned to Ari. "I can tell you he was not talking about sitting on the bench and if Jeff had heard him, I'm pretty sure he'd be flat on the ground right now."

Covering her mouth, Ari gagged. "Ewe. Gross. Yuk! Who says something like that to a married woman with her husband nearby? And a pregnant woman at that."

A look of horror swept across her face. She spun on her heels and pointed to me. "What in the fuck, Heather!"

"What?"

"They're swingers!"

I laughed and shook my head. "Have you gone mad? What makes you think they're swingers?"

Her mouth was wide open and her eyes looked like they were about to pop out of her head. "Think about it! The things they've been saying. The way Alison keeps flirting with Gunner and Jeff, and Grant doesn't say a damn word. He asked Ellie a few minutes ago if she's excited. She had no idea what he was talking about and just shrugged and said yes! They think we're swingers!"

Josh laughed as he started up the trail and we followed alongside him. "Okay, hold on. Maybe we're reading this all wrong. Heather, did they say anything to you at all?"

My eyes widened in horror. "No! Do you honestly think if they had told me they were swingers I'd even go to their campsite? I didn't even invite them on this hike— they invited themselves. I wanted to get away from her because she was flirting with you."

"Ha!" Ari said as she shoved her finger in my face.

Pushing it way, I kept talking. "I mentioned the hike and Alison said she'd always wanted to … oh no." Heather's hands covered her mouth.

"What? Oh no, what?" Ari asked in a panicked voice.

I swallowed hard as I dropped my hands to my side. "Well, she giggled and told Grant she knew her vibe was straight on. I didn't know what she meant when she said it, so ... I didn't say anything. Then she started talking about sex positions with me on the way over to Jeff and Ari's campsite. She asked what my favorite was. I just laughed and didn't answer her. She told me during the art class that her and her husband had a very open relationship."

Josh stumbled back and I had to reach for him.

"She ... she asked you that and you didn't think it was strange, Heather?"

With a shrug, I said, "Yes, but that doesn't mean they are swingers. It simply means they have no problem talking about sex."

Josh groaned. Ari patted him on the back. "Let me handle this."

I tilted my head and glared at Ari. "There's nothing to handle. You're being crazy."

Drawing in a deep breath, Ari let it out. "After she mentioned this ... open relationship of theirs. What did you say?"

"Nothing," I replied with a shrug. "She asked how long Josh and I had been together and I told her. Then she asked if we did things together a lot as couples and I said we did everything together."

I gasped and my hands covered my mouth.

"And there it is," Ari said crossing her arms across her chest.

"Oh no. After I said that, she giggled and repeated *everything*?"

Heather stopped walking and covered her mouth. "Shit! Shit! Shit! I replied back, almost everything. Then Ellie turned to me and asked if we were switching partners tonight!"

Ari's face turned white and Josh groaned again. "Don't just stand there, Heather! What did you say?"

My heart was racing. "Well, I said yes because Ellie was talking about charades for Christ's sake. How was I supposed to know Alison would take that the wrong way!"

Ari chewed on her nail while walking back and forth.

My stomach was twisting and turning. "I'm going to be sick."

"It's okay, let's catch back up with them and we can get it all straightened out. Maybe we're all reading this wrong."

"Fuck that, Josh! That man thinks he is going to have sex with me! That's why he said this would be an adventure. He's never fucked a pregnant woman before. Oh no. Jeff will kill him. If he tries to touch me, Jeff. Will. Kill. Him. The last thing I need is for my children's father to get hauled off to jail because Heather doesn't know what an open relationship is!"

I leaned over and moaned. I was going to get sick.

Ari grabbed me by the arm. "No way are you going to get out of this one, Heather. You brought two psychos into our group; you are going to have to fix this."

"Me?" I cried out.

Stomping her feet, Ari answered, "Yes! We are at full capacity with our couples. You stepped outside the circle, and when I say you stepped outside, I mean you took one giant leap into crazyville and brought it back with you."

Anger zipped through my veins. "How was I supposed to know, Ari?"

"Stop being so goddamn naïve about everything, Heather."

"What? How in the hell was I supposed to know?"

Ari rolled her eyes and let out a fake laugh as she placed her hands on her hips. "Please. Jeff and I got a weird vibe from the very second they spoke to us. You didn't think it was strange for a woman you just met to ask you about your favorite sex position?"

Josh stepped between us. "That's enough. Standing here fighting isn't going to do anything. Let's get going before they get too far ahead. We aren't getting anywhere arguing with each other."

Lifting my chin, I replied, "Fine, but I think we'll see that this was all a misunderstanding." I knew the words I just said weren't true, but I wouldn't give Ari the satisfaction of knowing that.

"Uh-huh. Well okay then, I'll let you lead the way," Ari said as she motioned for me to walk ahead.

It didn't take us long to get up to the top of the trail. There was supposed to be an amazing lookout.

We rounded the corner and I came to a stop. Josh and Ari walked up and stopped next to me.

"Oh shit," Josh whispered.

Ari turned to me and slowly shook her head. "I think we can safely say, I was right and you were wrong."

I couldn't pull my eyes off the sight before me. There were no words I could form. Alison and Grant where all over each other. Their hands were under shirts, down pants, and they were kissing like they were putting on a show. Jeff, Gunner, and Ellie stood with their backs to them looking out over the lookout. Gus sat at Grant's feet just staring up at them, ready to pounce if need be. Clearly the others had no idea what was happening.

"Ari, not now. We've got a bigger issue to deal with," Josh mumbled.

"Yeah, the second Jeff and Gunner turn around and see this, all hell will break loose because they'll put two and two together fast."

Josh sighed. "Right, let's nip it in the bud now."

Ari and Josh quickly walked over to Alison and Grant as I stood there like a frozen statue. *How could I be so stupid? How could I have read this so wrong?*

Josh grabbed Grant and Ari took a hold of Alison and began walking them over to me. I quickly stepped back and around the corner. Josh pushed Grant back, causing him to stumble.

"What in the fuck do you think you're doing?"

Grant looked confused as his gaze went from Josh to Alison.

"Wait, Alison I thought you said they would be into this?"

Alison shrugged.

"I thought they would. Heather, you said you were switching partners tonight."

Finally breaking out of my dazed look, I shook my head to clear my thoughts and answered Alison. "I was talking about charades!"

"Dear Lord," Grant softly spoke.

Ari walked up to Grant and poked him on the chest. "Oh, I think you need to be including the holy ghost, and a few hail Mary's in on this one, dude. Did you really think you were going to screw a pregnant woman?"

"Well I mean, if you were going to be down with it, I was."

Snarling her lip, Ari reached up and slapped Grant across the face. "You sick bastard!"

I was starting to feel dizzy. Not to mention sick to my stomach again.

Josh gently pulled Ari back and guided her next to me. He drew in a breath and exhaled. "Grant, Alison, this group is not into that. And honestly, if Jeff or Gunner find out what you had planned, well, honestly I'd be afraid right now, Grant."

"Very afraid," Ari added.

Grant reached for Alison's hand. "I think we're going to head on back down and continue on by ourselves."

With a nod, Josh replied, "I think that's the smart thing to do."

Alison stopped in front of me and gave me weak smile. "I'm so sorry, Heather. I really liked you. I was so looking forward to our time together, and I'm sorry if I misread things."

I stood there in a state of utter shock. Ari leaned forward, pointed to my stunned expression, and said, "I think this should pretty much tell you your swinger radar is way off, folks."

Alison frowned, then turned and headed down the trail with Grant.

"Breathe, Heather," Josh whispered into my ear. I leaned over, placed my hands on my knees and forced air in and out.

"Holy shit. How did that happen? What just happened?"

Ari giggled. "Wow. That's one to store away in the ole memory box upstairs."

Josh laughed as Gunner, Ellie, and Jeff all came around the corner. Ellie looked around and asked, "Where did Grant and Alison go?"

Gus ran up to me and whined as he pawed me. "I'm okay, boy. I think."

Josh and Ari looked at me. "They um … decided we really weren't the type of friends they wanted to hang out with."

Ellie's head pulled back in shock. "Wow. They didn't even really know us to make that assessment."

Ari chuckled. "They knew enough to know we weren't the type of friends they normally hang with."

A sense of guilt rushed through my body. "Ells, I'm so sorry for what I said earlier. I really do want to be here, and I'm sorry I invited a strange couple into our group. This was our weekend. I don't want to spend it with anyone else but y'all."

I watched as tears filled her eyes. "No, I'm sorry. I acted like a child."

"No, I did."

"No, it was me who—"

Ari walked up and stood between us. "Oh, for the love of God! Both of you acted like dicks. Now, can we get on with this hike before I birth this child I'm carrying? The last hour is one I'd like to try and forget please."

Ellie and I both smiled then wrapped Ari up in a sandwich hug.

Ari sighed then said, "All right, that's enough sappy shit, let's get moving. I've got pork chops calling my name."

My stomach growled and everyone started laughing. As we walked off, Jeff reached for my arm and held me back.

"What's up?" I asked.

"So what really happened?" he asked with one brow arched.

I pulled my lower lip in while taking a deep breath. With a shake of my head, I replied, "Trust me, you don't want to know."

The look on his face told me he might have already known.

He shook his head and glanced over to the rest of the gang. "I knew they were different."

My eyes widened as my eyebrows lifted. "They were different all right."

As we started to walk, Jeff let out a chuckle. "Although, I really would have loved to have seen Gunner's reaction when Grant put the moves on Ellie. That would have been priceless."

Looking up at Jeff, I asked, "You knew?"

He laughed and wrapped his arm around my shoulder. "Dear sweet, Heather. When will you learn? Jeff knows all. He is wise. He is smart, and let's not forget, he is handsome as hell."

I couldn't help but laugh. As much as I didn't think I wanted to be on this trip, I quickly realized that there was no place I'd rather be.

Sixteen

GUNNER

The fire popped as I held Ellie in my arms while Josh, Ari, and Heather told us how they came to the conclusion that Alison and Grant were swingers.

With a shake of my head, I grunted. "If I had turned around and saw that, I'd probably had killed the bastard. Fucker talking to Ellie like that."

The vibration of Ellie's chuckle moved through my body. "I still can't believe it. I mean, what sick kind of person would want to sleep with pregnant women?"

"Hey!" Ari and Heather said at the same time.

"I take offense to that. I may be pregnant, but I'm still sexy as hell," Ari said with a wink.

Jeff raised his beer up and said, "I agree with that one hundred and ten percent."

"I swear, it took everything I had not to punch that guy's lights out," Josh stated.

With a tip of my baseball cap, I replied, "You're a better man than me, Josh Hayes, 'cause I'd have ripped his throat out."

Ellie glanced up at me and shook her head. "You're a lover, not a fighter."

"Not when it comes to you, Ells."

Her smile lit up her face. "I love you," she said as she reached up for a kiss.

I twisted my cap around and gently kissed her lips. "I love you more, sweetheart."

"Well, as much as I would love to sit around this fire and talk, this is the last night I have with my wife before we head back home. I'm getting me some sex."

Ari laughed as she slapped Jeff on the chest. "You still stink! There is no way I'm letting you near me."

Jeff cupped Ari's face within his hands. "Baby, no amount of stink can keep you away."

Scrunching her nose, Ari said, "There is ... trust me, baby. There is."

"Gunner?"

The sound of Ellie's voice filled my dream.

"Gunner! Wake up!"

I wrapped my arms around her tighter. "Mmm, baby you feel so good."

"That's the pillow you're holding, now wake up!"

My eyes opened and I sat up. "What's wrong?"

Ellie went to talk, but a loud crash outside our tent had both of us jumping.

"That! There's something outside the tent. You need to go see what it is."

With a half-hearted chuckle, I shook my head. "Hell no. I'm not getting skunked like Jeff did."

She tilted her head and gave me a look my mother or Grams would give me. "Really, Gunner?"

Another crash, this one louder.

"Get dressed and see what it is! Please!" Ellie pleaded.

I let out a frustrated groan. "Fine. But if I get skunked, I'm grabbing your ass and rubbing all over you."

Her teeth sunk into her lip. "I like the sound of that."

My dick jumped. "Damn, Ellie. Now I'm turned on."

"You started it!"

After pulling on jeans, my boots, and a shirt, I slowly unzipped the tent. Ellie was right on my tail. At least if I got sprayed, she was going down with me.

I was slowly inching out when I heard the small ice chest start to open. I pushed Ellie back into the tent when I saw the shadow of a person. I jumped out and went to grab them, but I kicked whatever it was that had fallen, causing them to spin around and shine their flashlight in my eyes. The next thing I felt was something sharp hitting my jaw.

Dropping to the ground, I swore I saw stars.

"Gunner!" Ellie screamed as she rushed over to me.

"Damn it! Gunner, I'm so sorry, but you scared me!"

I tried to focus my eyes on the person now leaning over me.

"Ari, what are you thinking sneaking over here like that?"

"I was thirsty and we didn't have any bottles of water."

I rubbed my jaw and said, "Jesus, why were you making all that noise?"

She shined the flashlight in my eyes, causing me to look away.

"The light, Ari!"

"Shit, sorry!" she said as she shined it out the other way.

"I wasn't making any noise. I literally just walked up a second ago."

My jaw was throbbing as I slowly sat up with Ellie's help. "Then who was making all that nose?"

A noise came from our right. The three of us all turned to face it.

"Ari, can you shine your light over at the picnic table?" I asked.

When she did, we all gasped at once.

"Don't anyone move," I whispered.

Ari's hand must have started shaking because the light was moving all over the place.

"This camping trip is cursed, I tell you," Ari whispered.

Ellie grabbed onto my arm and tried to whisper, but her voice shook with fear. "Is ... is that a mountain ... mountain li ... um ..."

I stood slowly and pushed both girls behind me.

"Lion. Yes, it's a mountain lion. Slowly get into the tent, both of you."

"Gunner, no! You can't stay out here alone," Ellie pleaded.

I could hear Ari getting into the tent.

"Ells, baby, I can't take my eyes off of her; I need you to get into the tent slowly. Please."

"O-okay. I love you."

My heart was pounding so loudly I could hardly hear her speak. "I love you too."

Moving slowly, Ellie finally got into the tent.

I lifted my hands above my head and shouted, "Go on! Get the hell out of here!"

"Well hell dude, I'm only trying to see what is taking Ari so long."

My head jerked to the right as I watched Jeff come walking up, a flashlight shining directly on me.

"Jeff, stop!"

He instantly stopped. "What's wrong?"

I lifted the flashlight more to show him the mountain lion.

"Holy fuck!" he shouted as he jumped back. "There's a mountain lion on the table."

"No shit. I'm trying to get her to leave, but she's just sitting there. Staring at me."

"How do you know it's a she?"

I rolled my eyes and let out a small sigh. "I don't, Jeff. I'm just saying she."

"What makes you say she though?"

I groaned. "I don't know for fuck's sake."

"Lift your hands over your head and yell at her … or him."

I choose to ignore Jeff as I attempted to intimidate the big cat again. "Go on! Get out of here! Ha!"

From the left side, I heard someone walking up. "What in the name of everything good in this world are you doing yelling out here, Gunner? Can we get one night of decent sleep?"

It was then the mountain lion decided she'd had enough.

"Josh, dude you better stop walking, there's a mountain lion making her way over to you."

The flashlight was still shining on the cat as she made her way over to Josh. I was stunned that he didn't seem the least bit scared. He started jumping up and down on the one leg that wasn't hurt, making some weird noise as he lifted his hands over his head. Josh made a quick jerking motion forward, causing the cat to stop. When he did it again, she turned around and quickly started to trot off. Jeff and I both looked at each other with stunned looks. We walked up to Josh, flashlights shining directly on him.

"Seriously, can you lower your lights, guys?"

I dropped mine some and came to a stop in front of him. "How in the hell did you spook her?" Jeff asked.

Josh laughed as he hit us both on the side of the arm. "No fear, gentlemen. I have no fear."

Turning, he started to walk back over to his campsite.

"Yeah right, Hayes. It's called luck!" Jeff called out.

Josh lifted his hand and waved off Jeff as he called out, "Josh the Magnificent, one. Mountain lion, zero."

Jeff let out a chuckle and said, "Great. I wonder how many years we're gonna hear about this?"

Seventeen

ELLIE

Gunner's hands moved gently over me, sending an instant warmth through my body.

"Hmm, you feel so good."

With a smile, I rolled over to face him. "We almost died last night."

He chuckled lightly. "Hardly. But she was a big cat."

"She was a lion! Not a cat!"

Gunner drew me in closer to his body. "That was something to tell our kids someday."

My finger moved lazily over his chest. "This is our last day here."

"Have you had fun?"

"I have," I said with a wide grin. "I could have done without Josh almost cracking his head open, the bad art project, the skunk, the lion, and not to mention the almost orgy yesterday."

Gunner let out a laugh. "Yeah, that was … different. Heather felt really bad."

"She should! It makes my skin crawl thinking about it. Blah."

"Well, Josh came to the rescue on that one as well."

A small chuckle escaped from my lips. "You know he is never going to let you and Jeff forget how he scared that mountain lion away."

Groaning, Gunner moved over me, causing me to lay flat on my back. "Tell me about it. The way he walked off like he was king of the world was only the beginning." He leaned down and rubbed his nose against mine as he pushed his hard length on me. "What concerns me more is how your damn dog slept through the whole thing."

We both turned and looked at Gus. He was asleep on his bed, all four paws up and snoring.

I shook my head as I gazed back up at Gunner.

He pushed into me again. "I really don't want to talk about Josh or the crazy folks we met yesterday, or even that damn dog."

My teeth captured my lip and I wiggled my brows. "What do you want to talk about?"

"Nothing. I want to make love to my wife before the air leaks out of this mattress."

"I haven't brushed my teeth yet."

His finger traced along my jaw. "I'm willing to take the risk if you are."

My stomach dipped. I loved this man so much and I each time we were together, I swore it felt like the first time.

"For the sake of the air in the mattress, I think we should skip brushing our teeth."

We both chuckled before our eyes met and that familiar feeling we shared with each other filled the tent.

"Drew," I whispered before he pressed his lips to mine. He slowly pushed inside of me, then retreated a bit, before pushing in further. It was a heavenly torture.

"More," I gasped while pulling him in more with my legs.

His lips moved softly across my neck. "Greedy little thing."

"When it comes to you, I am. I never can seem to get enough."

We were face to face again. Blue eyes staring back at one another. The magic in the air was undeniable. Gunner pushed completely in and remained still. I could feel him pulsing inside of me. Lifting my hips, I silently begged him to move.

"I love you so much, sweetheart. Each morning I wake and look at you sleeping so peacefully. I'm taken by how much my heart grows more with your love."

His whispered words had my body already trembling and he hadn't even moved yet. My fingers slipped through his hair with ease, urging him to kiss me. When his lips touched mine, we quickly got lost in one another. Gunner moved slowly at first. Our hands exploring each other softly, our kiss growing with urgency.

"Ellie," Gunner said as he moved faster. Harder. Driving my orgasm to the surface.

"So close," I whispered as the feeling grew more. "Drew, I'm going to come."

He pushed in deeper as he spoke against my neck. "Ellie, feels so good. Baby, I'm coming."

With each thrust forward, Gunner's body trembled. A low growl as he finally released himself into me.

When he finally stopped moving, he stayed inside of me. Cupping my face with his hands, he peppered me with kisses while my fingers traced over his arms.

"Let's stay like this all day," I said.

His warm breath tickled my ear. "Should I blow up the sinking mattress?"

It was then I realized how fast we were slipping toward the floor. "Oh, my gosh what happened?"

With a chuckle, Gunner replied, "I might have gotten a little crazy toward the end."

Gus jumped up and barked, causing both of us to let out a small yelp.

"Who's up and ready for breakfast?"

My eyes widened in shock while Gunner dropped his head and shook it. He slowly pulled out of me and got up.

"Knock knock, love birds. Are we up?"

"Yes, Ari! We're up!" I shouted.

"Jeff's got breakfast going. This is our last morning so rise and shine! Y'all have plenty of time to bump uglies later. Off to wake up Josh and Heather now! Chop chop!"

Gunner groaned while he slipped on a pair of sweats. "She's so lucky she didn't show up three minutes earlier."

I let out a giggle and quickly cleaned up before getting dressed.

After I washed up and brushed my teeth, I threw my hair in a ponytail and met Gunner outside the bathrooms.

"Ready?" he asked with that dimpled smile of his.

"Yes! Today is starting out to be a wonderful day."

Gus jumped up and down, trying to get Gunner to throw a stick. "Not now, boy."

His arm wrapped around my waist as we headed back to our tent. "Hmm, wonder why?"

I leaned my head against his arm. "Thank you for this morning. It was amazing."

Gunner kissed the top of my head. "I agree."

"As much as I've loved this trip, I miss Alex something awful."

"Same here. I can't wait to see her."

Gazing up at him, I couldn't help but smile. I loved how Alex already had Gunner wrapped around her little finger.

We dropped our things back at our tent and headed over to Jeff and Ari's site. Josh and Heather were already there. As we walked up, we heard Josh re-telling the story of the mountain lion last night.

"And it's started," Gunner said with a chuckle.

"Jesus, Mary, and Joseph, Hayes. The mountain lion keeps getting bigger. It wasn't *that* big," Ari said as she shoved a piece of bacon into her mouth.

Heather glanced up at us and smiled. "Good morning. Why Ellie, you certainly look beautiful this morning."

"I feel beautiful," I said as I kissed Jeff on the cheek. He gave me a wink and said, "Good morning, sis."

Sitting, I reached for a piece of bacon. I inhaled deeply. "Pancakes," I whispered.

"Not just any kind of pancakes. Chocolate chip with fresh strawberries."

My stomach growled as I watched a large plate of pancakes be placed in the middle of the table. By the time I picked up my fork and went to get a pancake, they were gone.

"What in the heck, y'all?" I asked as I looked at Heather and Ari.

"What? I'm feeding two other people," Heather said with a huge smile.

Ari on the other hand stood and put a pancake on my plate. "There ya go, Ells."

I glanced down at the one cake then back up at Ari. "One? You're only giving me one?"

With a shrug, she motioned over to Jeff with her head. "He's making more."

"Here, Ellie, got you some more."

Jeff placed two more pancakes on my plate. Heather and Ari were both eyeing them, causing me to slide down the picnic table away from their reach.

"Hey, it looks like she has more chips in hers," Ari called out to Jeff.

Spinning around, Jeff grabbed the chips and dumped them over Ari's food. "There. You've got more chips. Happy now?"

"Yes, I am." Her eyes widened as she looked up at Jeff. "What in the hell are you wearing?"

Everyone looked at Jeff. I couldn't help but start laughing. His T-shirt said,

Gunner stood and walked over to Jeff, hitting him on the back. "Now I get the diving symbol on the back of your shirt. Only you, Jeff. Only you."

Eighteen

JEFF

I walked into the stables and took a good look around. Taking in a deep breath, I smiled.

"Any man who draws in that deep of a breath must either work with horses, or really love them."

Turning, I smiled at the young blonde woman standing in the doorway of the stables. She for sure must work at the stables. She had on dusty jeans, boots that had seen a better day, and work gloves were sticking out of her back pocket.

"I guess you could say both," I answered.

Her face lit up with a wider smile. "I was hoping you'd say that. Is there something I can help you with?"

I shook my head. "Nah, just snuck down here to see if I could get a jump on picking out a horse."

"Ah, you must be going on the group trail ride. I'm Kris, I'll be one of the guides."

I tipped my hat. "Yes, ma'am I am in that group. So tell me, Kris, which one would you put a five-year-old on?"

She frowned. "I didn't see where there was going to be any young children on this ride."

I laughed. "There isn't, well unless you include Josh; he acts like he's five."

Giggling, she walked over to a stall. "This here is Peppermint. She's a very sweet and timid girl. Likes to lead the pack and set the pace which is usually a very slow pace."

My hand ran along her neck where she treated me with a couple of head bobs. "She's perfect."

The young lady leaned against the stall. I couldn't help but notice how she let her eyes roam over my body. "Excuse me for saying this, but you don't seem like the type of guy who needs a gentle horse. You look built to ride. Hard."

Well, all right then. She got right to the point and so will I.

"I wasn't looking for a horse for me, but for my wife who is pregnant. She's been on horses her whole life, but she has fallen and lost a baby before, so I want to make sure she is safe."

The girl's cheeks blushed. "I'm so sorry … about the baby and even more for my shameless flirting."

I lifted my hands. "It's all good."

"I'm really embarrassed. But in my defense, you're not a bad looking guy and it's early in the morning. We'll use that as my excuse."

Laughing, I shook my head and focused back on Peppermint.

"Is this your first?"

I motioned to go into the stall. "Yes, please go on in. She'll love the attention."

"To answer your question, this will be our second child. We have an eleven-month-old little boy. Luke is his name.

"How adorable. I love that name."

I lifted up each leg on Peppermint and checked out her shoes.

Kris walked up to Peppermint's stall. "I promise your wife is going to be safe. She's the best horse we've got."

"So this is where you snuck off to, huh?"

Peeking up, I saw Ari and Ellie standing there. "Hey, just thought I would come down and see the horses."

Ari narrowed her eyes at me. "Uh-huh. Have you personally checked each shoe on every horse in here?"

Kris laughed. "He was asking about a horse for you to ride."

The second Ari's hands went to her hips, I knew I was in for it.

"Jeff Johnson. I've been riding horses since I was little. I don't need you treating me like I'm a piece of glass."

Kris took a few steps back as she looked between Ari and me. "I think I'll go ahead and start getting ready for the ride."

"Ari, I'm not treating you like a piece of glass. I love you and I love our baby. I'm being careful. That's all."

The stern look on her face instantly melted away. Making her way into the stall, she kissed me tenderly before giving Peppermint attention.

"She is a beautiful girl, isn't she?" Ari said with a wide grin.

Peppermint bobbed her head, causing all of us to laugh.

"Smart too," Ellie said.

"If y'all want to help round up the horses, I won't say no to the help. We're two people down today."

"I'd love to help," Ellie answered as she walked over to Kris.

Ari quickly gave Peppermint a kiss on the nose, turned and said, "Count us in too."

We'd been out on the trail for over an hour, and I was pretty sure each of us was in heaven. There was nothing like being on the back of horse and seeing some beautiful Texas country. I could ride all damn day and look at this country side.

Kris rode up front with Ari and Peppermint, while Tripp, the other guide, brought up the rear. He and Gunner instantly hit it off. Tripp had grown up on a cattle ranch in Leakey, Texas. He was helping out the owners of the stables for a few weekends until their son recovered from a bull riding accident.

"You say you have a ranch in Mason?" Tripp asked.

Gunner smiled. "Yes, sir. Been in my family since my great-great-granddaddy."

Tripp nodded. "My family's been raising Longhorns in Leakey since 1884. My dad got eighty thousand for a cow at auction last year."

"Holy shit," Gunner and I both said at once.

Laughing, Tripp took off his hat and wiped his brow before placing it back on. "Elite genetics, gentleman. My great-great-granddad knew what he was doing. We've got some Black Angus and Herefords as well. But mostly Longhorns."

Ellie let out a very loud groan before turning back to Gunner. "I know you could talk cattle all day, Gunner, but can we leave the shop talk out please. I just want to enjoy what's around us."

Gunner gave my sister a wide smile. "No more shop talk." He rode his horse alongside Ellie and they moved slightly away from the rest of us.

"Y'all are a great group of people. Been friends for a while?" Tripp asked.

I glanced around at everyone. Ari and Kris were lost in a conversation as were Josh and Heather.

"I've known Gunner and Josh since college. The girls have known each other longer."

"Wow, and you all ended up together as couples? That's pretty cool."

Focusing back on Tripp, I grinned. The kid couldn't have been but eighteen years old. "It is cool. For a while, it didn't look like we would all end up together like we did, but in the end … love won."

Tripp's mouth rose into a wide smile. "I think that's pretty damn cool. It's also great to see y'all out here, enjoying some time together."

I nodded as I looked out over my friends again.

"Yeah. It is pretty damn cool."

Nineteen

ARI

Ellie, Heather, and I all walked down to the river after we had gotten back from the trail ride. The guys were packing up the last of things while we decided to go for one more peek at the water. Ellie was abnormally quiet and Heather was the one chatting it up as we walked up and found a spot to sit.

I laid out the blanket and kicked my shoes off.

Ellie and Heather followed my lead.

"How are y'all feeling?" Ellie asked as she sank down onto the blanket.

"I'm actually feeling pretty darn good. This weekend was exactly what I needed. Thank you, Ellie, for pushing us into it."

Ellie grinned. "It was really more Jeff's idea. I'm glad we did it though."

Her smile faded and she looked away. Sitting up, I took her hand in mine. "Ells, what's going on?"

With a shrug, she turned to look at us both. "I guess I'm worried this is it. That once you both have the babies, our friendship will kind of take a backseat."

"What?" Heather said as she moved closer to us and took Ellie's other hand.

My chest felt tight. I knew exactly how Ellie felt because I'd been feeling the same way.

"Truth be told, I've already expressed my concerns to Jeff. I don't want to give up times like this, but once we all have kids, will we still be able to do stuff like this?"

Heather squeezed both Ellie and mines hand. "Apart from my moment of insanity this weekend, I can honestly say you two mean so much to me. But, things are going to change. They already have. We made this weekend work; we'll make another one work. The great thing about this is we can still do things together, but now we can do them with our kids."

A tear slipped slid down my cheek. "I want our kids to all grow up together."

"They will," Heather said with a smile. "They're going to grow up loving each other and being the best of friends. They'll fight." Heather winked at us then scrunched up nose up. "They'll be the best of friends and probably get into a lot of trouble together."

Ellie giggled. "Especially if you have a boy, Heather. Him and Luke, I can see it now if they are anything like their fathers."

We all laughed. Ellie took in a deep breath and exhaled.

"Ells," Heather said with that sweet smile of hers.

"I just love you both so much, I don't ever want to lose what we have. I don't want it to change."

I stood up and motioned for Ellie and Heather to stand up. "We've been friends a long time. Been through a lot together and I know the future is going to hold a lot of laughter, tears, and most likely a few arguments."

I took both of their hands in mine. "But the one thing that will never change is us."

We all embraced in a hug and started laughing when Heather's pregnant belly nearly touched mine.

My heart felt full and I knew deep down inside, nothing important would ever change. I'd always have these women by my side through thick and thin.

"I love you bitches," I said through a sob.

Ellie sniffled and hugged me tighter. "I love you too, Ari."

Heather pulled back and looked into my eyes. "I love you to infinity."

We hugged for a few more minutes before we got our emotions under control.

Sitting back on the blanket, we talked about baby rooms and Heather's wedding. The whole time I couldn't help but think about Jeff's promise of coming back to the state park with our kids and their kids.

With a smile, I filed this spot deep within my heart. The three of us would sit in this spot again one day; I believed it deep within the depth of my soul.

I leaned back and let the warm Texas sun hit my face as I listened to Heather and Ellie argue about what would be the best way to set up the chairs on the beach for Heather's wedding. With a smile, I listened to them go on and on.

This is what life was all about and I'd never take it for granted. Every smile, tear, and angry word spoken. It all shaped us into who we were and who we would become.

Twenty

GUNNER

My heart felt heavy as I shut the tailgate on my truck. The weekend was over and we'd all be heading back to reality.

"You all right, Gunner?"

Josh's voice pulled me from my thoughts.

"Yeah, I'm fine. A little sad to see the weekend ending. It's been fun hanging out like old times."

Josh nodded and blew out a deep breath. "Things are really going to change in a few months."

I smiled and hit his back. "Especially for you, dude. You're getting married in a few weeks, babies on the way this summer. Your world is about to be turned upside down."

He frowned and snarled his lip. "Gee, thanks for the pep talk there, Gunner."

"Keeping it real my friend, keeping it real."

"You both packed up and ready to go?" Jeff asked as he made his way over to us.

"I think so. The next time we want to do a weekend getaway, I vote for somewhere warm, with a place on the beach and comfortable beds," Josh said as he rubbed his lower back.

"Too much sex on the blow-up?" Jeff asked with a straight face.

Rolling his eyes, Josh gave Jeff a dirty look. "You could probably have sex anywhere, I swear."

Jeff nodded. "My goal someday is sex on a horse."

Josh and I both stared at Jeff. Pinching my brows, I asked, "Sex on a horse. With Ari?"

"Well certainly not with the fucking horse, Gunner. Yes, with Ari. What in the hell, dude?"

Tossing my head back, I laughed then punched Jeff on the arm. "Hell, you don't really know with you, Johnson."

Josh chuckled as we made our way over to the girls. "Think they had fun?" Josh asked.

"Well I don't know about you two, but I made sure my wife had a good time. At least when we were alone I did."

"Jesus, Jeff. Is that all you think about is sex?" Josh asked.

"Yes," Ari answered as she turned and looked at us. "Ninety-nine percent of the time."

Jeff pulled Ari to him and kissed her on the lips. "And you love it."

She rubbed her stomach. "I must if I'm pregnant again with your baby."

Heather seemed to melt into Josh as he held her close to him. She looked up at Josh then over to Ellie and smiled. "I'll be the first to admit I wasn't so sure about this trip, but I've had a blast. I miss my bed, but it's been a nice break from reality."

I motioned with my finger for Ellie. She stood and walked into my arms. Her warm body brought mine to life. Standing on her toes, she kissed me gently then said, "This has been so much fun, but I miss Alex."

Ari let out a sigh of relief. "I've been almost on the verge of tears I miss Luke so much."

"I can't wait to see the little guy," Jeff added.

I looked around at my best friends and felt a peace settle into my chest. I wasn't sure when the next time we would be able to sneak off like this for a weekend would be, but I made a promise to myself that I would make sure we had small moments like this. Just us, being us.

Ellie turned in my arms and faced everyone else as we stood in a circle. Turning my attention on Josh and Heather, I said, "So, in a few weeks we're marrying off the last two of the gang."

Heather's face lit up as did Josh's. "I'm ready. More than ready, honestly," Josh said as he placed his hands over Heather's swollen belly.

Looking up at Josh, Heather softly said, "I'm counting down the days."

We stood there in silence. It was almost like no one really wanted to leave, but I knew we were all ready to get home and get settled back into life.

"I guess we should head back," Jeff said first. "But there is one thing I want to do before we go."

Ellie looked at her brother and asked, "What's that?"

With a smile, he looked at each of us, one at a time. "I want us all to stand here and make a promise to each other that someday we'll return to these campsites with our kids and their kids."

Ari wiped a tear from her face.

I nodded. "I'm all about that promise, Jeff."

"Same here, I think that's a great idea," Josh said as he leaned down and kissed Heather's forehead.

We all turned and faced the river. Before I knew it, we stood in a line, our arms all wrapped around the person next to them as we looked out over the scenery.

"What do you think it will be like?" Ellie asked with a wide grin. "I can't help but wonder how many kids each of us will have and how many kids they'll have. Will they grow up and move away or stay close by us?"

"I'm going to say, after this, I'm think we'll stick to the two we're having," Heather said with a light sigh.

Everyone laughed.

Ari peeked up to Jeff. "I think two sounds about right for us as well."

Ellie dropped her head against my shoulder. "Two seems to be the magic number. If we're blessed with another baby, I won't argue."

"Then it's settled. Someday we'll be back with the whole gang here at this park," Jeff said putting his hand out. We each placed our hand over the others as we formed a circle.

"To the promise," Ari said with a wide grin.

Five voices all responded at once.

"To the promise."

TWENTY SOME YEARS LATER...

"I'm so excited I could scream."

I chuckled and took Ellie's hand. "So am I, sweetheart. We've been waiting a long time for this to happen."

"We sure have. I can't believe we were able to get the same campsites. It was smart of Jeff to call up last year and reserve all of them. And we got them all in that same area. I can't wait to see the kids playing."

Reaching for her hand, I brought it up and kissed the back of it. My heart was filled with an unbelievable happiness. "It's going to be a great weekend."

I pulled into the same campsite we had camped at over twenty years ago. "It looks the same."

Ellie chuckled. "Do you remember the mountain lion?"

"Yes, and don't remind Josh. It took that bastard fifteen years before he finally stopped telling that story."

"Trust me, I won't have to remind him … he already mentioned to it Heather the other day. She told me."

Rolling my eyes, I got out of the truck. "Great."

We both stood and looked at the campsite and then glanced back to the fifth-wheel we had bought a few years back. "I'm glad we wised up a few years back and gave up tent camping."

Ellie nodded in agreement. "You know, Anissa's going to want to spend the night with us."

That warm feeling settled in my body like a soft blanket. "And that's totally fine with me."

Laughing, Ellie shook her head. "That little girl has you wrapped around her finger. Lauren told me about the pony."

"She wanted it!"

With her hands on her hips, Ellie tilted her head and gave me that look. The one where she was right and I was wrong, and she wanted me to admit it.

"Fine, maybe I shouldn't have bought it without talking to Colt and Lauren first, but Hunter, Bayli, and Joshua all have a horse. Why couldn't Anissa?"

"You make a good point on that, but next time, save something like that for Christmas or her birthday. And for goodness sakes, talk to the kids first, Gunner."

I took Ellie's hand in mine. "Duly noted. Looks like Jeff and Ari are over there; let's head on over."

"You don't want to set up the RV?"

"Nah, we'll do it in a minute."

As we made our way over to Jeff and Ari's RV, Ari came walking out with her arms filled with bags of chips.

"Need help?" Ellie asked as she walked up.

"Yes! Thanks! It's about time y'all got here. Everyone is here and in the spot."

"The spot?" I asked.

Ellie looked up at me. "Yes, it's the place Ari, Heather, and I spent those last few hours while you guys were packing up."

"Ah," I said nodding my head. Taking a few bags from Ari and Ellie, we started walking down to the river.

"Everyone is here you said?" Ellie asked Ari.

"Yes, and I'm pretty sure each of our kids loaded our grandchildren up with sugar. They are all over the damn place."

Ellie and I chuckled. As we got closer, my eyes scanned the area and took it all in.

"Good lord, look at them all," Ellie said with a giggle.

Ari came to a stop. "Look who finally showed up."

Each of our friends turned and greeted us warmly. Brad and Amanda held a sleeping Mason in their arms. "Hey, y'all. About time you got here!" Amanda said with a smile.

Jeff stood and took the bags of chips from Ellie and Ari and tossed them onto the portable table that was set up with snacks and drinks.

He reached out and shook my hand. "Gunner, you guys need help with the RV?"

"Nah, damn thing practically sets itself up."

Josh stood up next to Jeff and reached for my hand. "Hey, Josh. Heather. Y'all get everything set up?"

Josh and Heather had bought their RV only a few weeks back and this was the first time they had used it. "The hardest part about it was driving with that bitch on my bumper. Give me a trailer with ten horses in it and I'm fine, but that damn thing nearly wrecked us four times."

Heather rolled her eyes. "It did not. He did great with it and you're right, it practically sets itself up."

Scott stood next and shook my hand. "Gunner, long time no see."

I chuckled and hit him on the back. "I saw you yesterday. And no, I still don't want to sell you that stud so don't ask."

Holding up his hands in surrender, Scott laughed. "I wasn't going to ask. But if you change your mind, I'm willing to offer a good price."

Jessie stood and kissed Ellie on the cheek then gave me a hug. "Did y'all see Anissa lost another tooth?"

Ellie gasped. "She did! Oh, that sweet baby girl."

Ari pulled out two more chairs. "Here, have a seat. This is the prime location to watch the action."

Ellie and I sat next to Josh and Heather. The grandkids were running everywhere. I couldn't help but notice how all of our kids were gathered around a few blankets closer to the river, talking, laughing, and tossing back a few beers. Every now and then you would hear one of them shout out to the kids.

"Trey, get off Mireya."

"Charlotte, don't put mud down Anissa's swimsuit."

Tears threatened to spill from my eyes as I watched the kids we had raised raising their own little ones. "Look at them. It's like looking in a mirror," I said.

Ellie reached for my hand and squeezed it. "Do you remember how we stood here and worried that we would drift apart? Look at this. Not only did we *not* drift apart, but our kids all ended up with each other. Of course, a couple added to the family."

Laughter filled the air until a silence settled among us. I turned and looked at each one of my best friends. They were more than friends. They were my family. Not all of them stood in this spot and made that promise all those years ago, but when we told them about it, they vowed to hold the promise as well. And we did. As crazy as it was to get everyone's schedules to work, we made it happen. My heart felt full. I was positive nothing would ever top this day.

I stood and opened up the ice chest and grabbed two drinks, a beer for me and a bottled sweet tea for Ellie. Handing her the tea, I cleared my throat. Everyone turned their attention on me.

Trying to talk, my voice cracked, causing me to pause for a moment and regroup. I was overcome with emotion and I knew the rest of the gang was as well. "We did it. We all went through times of happiness, sadness, anger, and fear, but son-of-a-bitch, we did it. There isn't a day that doesn't go by where I don't lay my head down at night and thank God for each of you. You're more than friends, you're family."

I turned and looked down at the river. Alex looked up at us and lifted her hand and waved. That prompted each of our kids to do the same.

There was no doubting how blessed we were.

I lost the battle and a single tear trickled down my face.

Ellie stood next to me and wrapped her arm around my waist. It didn't take long for everyone else to stand. We all stood there, arms wrapped around each other, like we did all those years ago when we looked out over the same view and dreamed about our future.

Looking up at me, Ellie's blue eyes shined with happiness. I was instantly swept into a memory from so many years ago. A young, beautiful, brown-haired, blue-eyed girl sitting next to me on my sofa watching *Cars*. I knew that day she would own my heart.

"This is what we wanted all those years ago when we made that promise. Happy kids, happy grandkids, and one hell of a happy and blessed life."

My voice cracked as I looked back out at our family. "This sight before us … this is it. All we wanted right before our eyes."

"To the promise," Jeff softly said.

We all repeated at once, "To the promise."

It's never the end … only the beginning of the next story.

To everyone who has supported me over these last four years! THANK YOU! I couldn't do this without the amazing readers, bloggers, and friends who support me with each and every book.

Wanted Series

Wanted
Saved
Faithful
Believe – novella
Cherished
A Forever Love
The Wanted Shorts
All They Wanted – novella

Entire series on Audiobook except for *All They Wanted*

Love Wanted in Texas Series (Wanted spin off series)

Without You
Saving You
Holding You
Finding You
Chasing You
Loving You

Entire series on Audiobook

Broken Series

Broken
Broken Dreams
Broken Promises
Broken Love

First three books on Audiobook

Journey of Love Series

Unconditional Love
Undeniable Love
Unforgettable Love

Entire series on Audiobook

Speed Series

Ignite
Adrenaline

With Me Series

Stay With Me
Only With Me (coming 1.31.17)

Boston Love Series

Searching for Harmony
Fighting for Love (coming 4.4.17)

Stand Alones

The Journey Home
Who We Were (Available on Audiobook)
The Playbook (Available on Audiobook
Made for You

Coming Soon

Fated Hearts Series

Heart in Motion (Coming 6.27.17)
Guarded Hearts (Coming 7.25.17)

Seduced Series

Seduced (Coming 9.12.17)

Joint Projects

Finding Forever (Co-written with Kristin Mayer)
Stories for Amanda

Young Adult – writing as Ella Bordeaux

Beautiful
Forever Beautiful (coming March 2017)

Printed in Great Britain
by Amazon